Copyright © 2024 by John Chambers

All rights reserved.

No part of this publication may be reproduced, distributed, or transmitted in any form or by any means, including photocopying, recording, or other electronic or mechanical methods, without the prior written permission of the publisher, except as permitted by U.K. copyright law. For permission requests, contact planetbizarropress@gmail.com

The story, all names, characters, and incidents portrayed in this production are fictitious. No identification with actual persons (living or deceased), places, buildings, and products is intended or should be inferred.

Book Cover by Ash Ericmore

Old man Icon by Icon8

Cursing Home

John Chambers

Planet Bizarro Press

Author's Note

In most stories in which a character learns they have special powers, this revelation occurs during childhood. For this book, I wanted to answer the question, "What if the opposite were true?" What if characters developed magical abilities when they were senior citizens? How would society treat them? I bet not much better than how we treat them now. Their magic would just be another thing people would try to exploit. Everything would be the same except for one minor detail: these old folks would have the power to fight back.
—JC

FOR GRANDPA

Chapter One

Grandpa Earnest awakes to 50,000 volts surging through him in a ruthless vortex of pain. Muscles he hasn't used in decades go rigid. He spasms, convulses, flops out of bed and lands face-first on the hardwood.

"Time to go, Dad," Julie says, grinning madly.

She sets the taser aside, grabs his ankles, and drags his wiry frame toward the bedroom door, grunting with the effort. Earnest tries to speak but manages only the guttural moan of a sick cow that's about to be shot. He leaves a trail of drool along the floor like a slug marking its path. As he passes by the corner bedpost, he finds enough strength to reach out and grab hold of it.

Julie pulls harder. "Let go, Dad."

"Noooo," he manages to say.

Arica bursts into the room.

"What the hell, Mom?" she says in a gravelly voice. Arica's vocal cords are damaged because she once tried to kill herself by drinking bleach.

"I'm glad you're here, sweetie," Julie says. "Be a good girl and stomp on your grandpa's hands."

Arica looks down at him. She can't believe this day has finally come. As foolish as it is, she always thought there would be more time.

Earnest snarls up at her while fighting to keep hold of the bedpost. He can't stand the look of pity on her face.

"Is this really necessary?" Arica asks her mom.

"You know it is, sweetie. Now, do as your mother says and *get to stomping.*"

Arica sighs and steps over to where Earnest is holding on. She winces and says, "I'm so sorry, grandpa." She rears up and digs the heel of her boot into his wrist. He yelps but still refuses to let go, so Arica smashes his fingers. He cries out as his grip breaks.

Julie giggles while dragging her father the rest of the way into the living room. This is the greatest day of her life. Not so much for Earnest, of course. He's dreaded this day ever since Julie revealed her plans to get rid of him. He kept thinking Arica would convince her mom to change her mind, while Arica prayed the problem would go away if she just ignored it hard enough.

Julie drops his feet, then steps over to the coffee table and picks up a roll of duct tape. Arica watches, stomach uneasy, as her mother binds Earnest's wrists and ankles. Arica cringes with each cinch of tape.

"Please," he croaks. "It was just one demon."

"That *one* demon you summoned killed two children," Julie says. "Do you know how many angry calls I received? No, you don't. You were too busy being useless. Eating our food. Breathing our air."

"He didn't mean to do it," Arica says. "It was an accident."

"Yes, an accident," Earnest echoes. "It won't happen again."

Julie crouches beside him. "Dad, I need you to hear what I'm saying. It's time for you to go. I planned to get rid of you even before the demon incident. But when you developed powers, I got to put you on the priority list. We have a reservation with your new forever home, and I don't want to be late." She kisses him on the cheek.

The vein in Earnest's forehead swells. "You ungrateful trollop! I raised you, and this is the thanks I get?"

"You raised me because that's what you were legally required to do. Why should I thank you for doing your job?" Julie stands and stretches her back. She wonders why oldies can't go quietly like they're supposed to. "Besides, I would be negligent in my duty as a good citizen if I didn't dump you off."

Earnest fixes Arica with a pained stare. "Arica, my little bonbon. You don't really want to see your grandpa taken away, do you?"

Arica's head droops. "I—"

"It's not up to her, Dad," Julie says. "And shame on you for dragging your granddaughter into this."

Earnest scowls. "Shame on me? How about shame on you?" He struggles against his bonds. This is his last chance to get through to Julie. He's got to make one last push to convince her that what she's doing is wrong. "How could you do this to me? Your own flesh and blood. You deserve to—"

Julie cuts him off by slapping a piece of duct tape over his mouth. "That's better," she says.

Earnest shoots them a murderous look. Arica stares at her feet to avoid meeting her grandpa's gaze. She releases a breath when the doorbell rings.

"I'll get it," Arica says as she bolts for the door. She opens it and finds Toby standing there. His face lights up when he sees her. Though Arica is a senior in high school and Toby a junior, they are best friends. He follows her around like a puppy dog, lapping up whatever praise Arica throws his way. He's had a crush on her for as long as he can remember. She makes him feel funny inside—a strange combination of fire and ice. Like being immersed in a hot tub filled with popsicles.

"Your gramps ready to go?" Toby asks.

Arica frowns and glances behind her. "My mom is ready for him to go."

She moves out of the way and Toby takes a tentative step inside. When he sees Earnest subdued on the floor, his intestines churn. He hates conflict of any kind and does his best to avoid it. Arica notices his discomfort and is instinctually repelled by it. But it also gives her a certain delight because it means she can manipulate him.

"Can you help my mom with him?" Arica says. "I'd rather not."

"Of course," Toby says as his tension drains. "I'm always here for you."

Toby and Julie drag Earnest outside the house and over the gravel walkway. He grimaces in pain as jagged pebbles slice into his tired flesh, his t-shirt and boxers offering little protection.

Once they get to Julie's car, Toby opens the back door and the two of them toss Earnest across the seats. He's so tall that he has to raise his knees almost to his chest to avoid getting his ankles broken when Toby slams the door shut.

Julie dusts her hands and lets out a contented sigh. "Well, that wasn't so bad."

Arica says something from the front of the house, but the wind muffles her scratchy voice. Toby's ears perk up and he scampers over to her, willing and ready to cater to whatever she might need.

"What was that?" he asks.

"I said, can't we at least let him get dressed first?"

Toby squishes his eyebrows together. He looks over his shoulder toward the car, then back at Arica. "Why would he need clothes?"

Arica chuffs. "Because he's a human being?"

Toby scratches his head. "I guess we could ask your mom."

Arica chews her bottom lip as Julie saunters up to them. "Ready to go, kids?"

"What about Grandpa's clothes?" Arica asks.

Julie snaps her fingers. "I knew I was forgetting something."

Arica blinks. She wonders how her mother failed to notice that Earnest isn't dressed.

Julie smiles at Toby. "Could you be a dear and fetch the suitcase in the living room? I packed up some of my dad's junk last night."

"Sure thing," Toby says. He runs back into the house to retrieve the suitcase. Helping Arica's mom is the next best thing to helping Arica.

Arica says, "No, I meant Grandpa's not wearing clothes right *now*."

Julie waves her off. "Christ, it's not like he's going to a job interview." She pauses and laughs. "Not that anyone would hire him. Your grandpa's *skills* aren't exactly in demand."

Arica watches her indignant grandpa through the car window. His nostrils flare as he draws in rapid breaths.

Arica says, "There must be someone in need of a printing press operator. What about—"

"Have you been falling asleep in class again, dear? No one uses paper anymore except the oldies." She pats Arica on the head. Hopefully, the poor child will understand one day.

Toby emerges from the house carrying Earnest's suitcase. Though Arica's not sure if it really qualifies as a suitcase. It's more like a satchel. It looks like its previous owner abused it for its long, painful life, then left it for dead in a garbage dump before Julie resurrected it.

"What about the rest of his things?" Arica asks.

"Don't worry," Julie says. "I'll eBay the good stuff and get rid of the rest with a garage sale."

"You can't sell his things!"

"I can and I will. And you'll stop complaining if you enjoy receiving an allowance."

Toby pretends to examine a cloud while Arica bristles. She's offered to get a job on numerous occasions, but her mother always refuses. Julie says Arica should concentrate on her schoolwork instead of being an uppity, money-hungry brat.

"You're afraid of my independence," Arica says.

"You know what happens when I give you freedom? You try to whiten your insides with bleach." Julie turns her back on her daughter and opens the driver-side door.

Arica clenches her fists. Why does her mom always bring that up? Toby reaches out for her, but she steps away before he can touch her.

Arica walks around the hood and squeezes into the back seat next to Earnest. She crams herself against the door to give her grandpa more room. She peels back the duct tape from the corner of Earnest's mouth to help him breathe. Toby shakes his head and gets in the front seat.

As Julie pulls out of the driveway, Arica looks up and sees all the neighborhood activity. It surprises her she didn't notice it before.

Grandmas and grandpas are being dragged from their homes and shoved into waiting vehicles. Other families use wheelbarrows, dollies, or purloined shopping carts. Some old people go willingly. Others have to be restrained. There are grandparents in chains, hogtied grandparents, and grandparents wearing burlap sacks. Other grandparents are zip-tied, surrounded by layers of rope, bound with extension cords to makeshift stretchers, or rendered unconscious with massive doses of horse tranquilizer.

Today is National Dump Off Your Old People Day, an epic celebration that binds communities together by their most valued trait—their youth. Other holidays are but pale shadows that provide only a tiny fraction of the happiness of this joyous occasion.

Julie motors down the street, careful not to run anyone over. She's not too worried about striking an oldie, but hitting one of their family members would be a tragedy. People are escorting their old folks to the bus stop for transport to one of several facilities that specialize in caring for magic-inclined seniors. You can sometimes get rid of an oldie who hasn't yet developed powers, but it's harder to get on the preferred list.

From the front seat, Toby twists his face with concern. He keeps glancing behind him to see Arica scowling.

"Stop staring at me," Arica says.

"Sorry," Toby says over the top of his seat. "Are you mad at me?"

"I will be if you keep asking."

Toby considers for a moment. "Is it because of your grandpa? You have to know this is for the best."

Arica cranes her neck at him. "And why do I have to know that, Toby? My grandpa is a kind and decent person. He taught me how to ride a bike, and he helps me with my homework."

"You're the smartest kid in school. You don't need a doddering old fool holding you back."

"I heard that, you prick," Earnest says through the peeled corner of duct tape.

Julie has noise-canceling headphones on, listening to a podcast on home remodeling. She always wears headphones when riding with family.

"Nobody's talking to you, oldie," Toby says.

Earnest glares at the boy while Arica kicks the back of Toby's seat.

"Don't be a jerk," she says.

Toby wrings his hands. What he said about Arica is true. The smartest students are the ones who teach themselves. Most of the teachers in school are young and inexperienced, because the oldest are shipped off to nursing homes at the earliest opportunity. Children are often left to fend for themselves if they want to learn.

"Why are you sticking up for him?" Toby asks. "Your grandpa is a murderer."

"I know what he is!" snaps Arica.

Toby wants to change the subject, but his mind goes blank. It always does when Arica gets upset. All he can think about is the tightness in his chest.

Julie slams on the brakes just in time to avoid pancaking a family crossing the street. A wife-and-husband team is escorting two sets of grandparents. They have collars around their necks attached to long poles. Toby looks on with admiration.

"Why didn't your mom think of that?" he asks Arica.

Arica sighs. "She did, but by the time she called Animal Control, they were out of collars."

Toby nods. There are chat forums where people discuss the best ways to transport oldies. It's been two years since his parents dumped his granny. Back then, straightjackets were all the rage.

They drive on and reach the bus depot. Grimy buses are lined up end-to-end along the street as far as they can see. Electronic marquees on the back of the buses announce which facilities they are destined for. They have names like Best Years Past, Done and Discarded, Fantastic Forever Homes, and Thrown-Away Key. Wary guards armed with cattle prods shuffle old folks aboard. If a grandma or grandpa resists or otherwise holds up the line, they get juiced. A few of the buses are over capacity, so the guards strap the extras to the roofs with bungee cords.

Instead of stopping to offload Earnest, Julie drives on. She wants to make damn sure that he makes it to his destination, so she has elected to take him herself. She can also deal with any potential problems or clerical missteps with the reservation. She's not about to let sloppy work by a distracted intern result in her dad being returned and dumped on her porch.

Chapter Two

They drive by a massive billboard with a cartoon image of a woman tearing her hair out next to an older gentleman lying in bed. A thick chain binds the two of them together. The caption reads, "Oldies holding you back? Reclaim your life!" Underneath is a website—*www.deadweight.gov*.

After a few more miles, a banged-up sign comes into view. It reads, "Withered Oaks Retirement Community." Twelve-foot-high fences replete with angry barbed wire surround the complex. Each barb resembles a tiny spearhead, some with bits of dried flesh still attached. Julie pulls up to an open wrought iron gate. On each side are two lion statues, heads looking downward with jaws partially open. They're either roaring or submitting; it's impossible to tell.

Julie drives through the gate and around a vast, circular driveway. Balloons suspended in the air spell out "Dump Now!" A banner attached to the front of the building proclaims "Highest Rebate Guaranteed!"

The space in front of the entrance is already clogged with vehicles making deliveries of old people, so Julie parks some distance away. She leaps out of the car and surveys the grounds. Tall weeds poke through cracked pavement. Piles of uncollected trash decay in the corners. Broken glass and discarded coffee cups litter the walkway leading to the front door.

"This reminds me of when I dumped my mother," Julie says to no one in particular.

Arica gets out of the car and frowns.

Julie continues, "As fun as this is, there's nothing quite like your first dump. It's exhilarating and satisfying and you'll relive it over and over." She glances at Arica. "You'll understand when the time comes for you to dump me."

Arica says nothing. She turns and stares at the imposing structure before them. The paint on the old brick building is peeled, cracked, and streaked with dark stains. Lattice archways choked with overzealous ivy bracket the way to the front door. A van with blue candy stripes sits near the entrance. It has cut deep tracks into the scraggly lawn. A man with greasy black hair is unloading jars of milk.

Julie uses a pair of cuticle trimmers she has stashed in her purse to free Earnest from his bonds. He takes several deep breaths while massaging his sore wrists. He considers making a run for it, but he knows he wouldn't make it far before being tackled or tased.

Julie escorts her reluctant father up the sidewalk while Arica and Toby follow. Arica absently adjusts her turtleneck. She always wears a turtleneck to hide the deep scar around her neck from when she tried to hang herself.

As they near the entrance, Arica gets a better look at the milkman. His face is gaunt and drawn, like he once got his chin stuck in a vacuum cleaner. His eyes are beady yet sharp, and they betray intense intelligence. Arica can't decide if it's the kind of intelligence used for academic study or dismembering corpses. His nametag identifies him as Wilford.

An orderly drags a sobbing old man through sliding glass doors while his family cheerfully waves goodbye. A woman in a green-gray pinstriped business suit scurries past him the other way and walks right up to Julie.

"Welcome to Withered Oaks," the woman announces. "I'm so happy to meet you! I'm Eloise, the administrator."

"I'm Julie. We spoke on the phone about my worthless dad."

"Of course," Eloise says. "You've come to the right place."

Arica thinks that if this is the right place, she would hate to see the wrong place. Despite Eloise's friendly demeanor, she smiles like a snake.

"And you must be Earnest," Eloise says, making a duck face. She hunches over with her hands on her knees, even though Earnest looms over her. "That's such a quaint name you have. What if we call you something more fitting, like 'Dave'?"

Earnest sneers but says nothing. Eloise never tires of seeing the look on an oldie's face when they realize their situation is hopeless. Earnest still has fire in his eyes, but Eloise knows he'll break within the hour.

Julie says, "I think that's a splendid idea."

"Me too," Toby says. "Earnest is a dumb oldie name." He looks at Arica to gauge her reaction to his quip. She punches him in the ribs. Toby lets out an exasperated grunt and rubs his midsection.

"My name. . . is *Earnest*." He fixes Eloise with the most defiant stare he can muster.

Eloise chortles. "Whatever you say, Dave." She straightens her posture and tugs at her jacket. She says to Julie, "Now, I understand your father is having memory problems?"

"There's nothing wrong with my goddamn memory," Earnest says.

"Mood swings too, I see," Eloise says. "No worries, we'll be watching him closely. Now, if you will all follow me."

They follow her toward the entrance. As they pass through the sliding glass doors, Arica glimpses Wilford the milkman pocketing a pair of needle-nose pliers.

When they step into the lobby, a noxious cloud of funk smacks them in their faces.

"Dear God, that is foul," Toby says, wrinkling his nose.

Arica glares at Toby for his rudeness, but she concedes the point. It smells like industrial-strength bleach is fighting a losing battle against an abhorrent miasma of vomit and diarrhea.

Eloise laughs. "All our new visitors react that way." Then she looks at Earnest and says, "Don't worry, you'll get used to it. Soon, it will just smell like home." She knows that's a lie, but it's a fun one.

Earnest sees right through her insincerity, and he shares the others' disdain for the air quality. "It smells like a damn sewer in here."

"Please do not speak unless spoken to," Eloise says. "It's one of our rules here."

"But you just spoke to him," Arica says.

Eloise gives her a patronizing smile, then leads them to the front desk. While Eloise checks Earnest in, Arica examines the surroundings. A 50-gallon fish tank against the left wall produces a soft bubbling sound. It's home to a single, listless betta fish with chewed fins and missing scales. To the right is an empty water cooler with pink mold growing on the drainage tray. To the left is a row of thinly padded seats. A few of them contain outdated magazines with foxed covers. A forlorn television with bleary colors hangs in a corner. A commercial comes on featuring a little girl and her mother. The girl asks, "Can we please go to Disney World this year, mommy? Pleeease!?"

The mother gives an exaggerated sigh. "I'd love to, honey, but we have to take care of Grandpa." The scene cuts to a shot of the woman's husband feeding mushy peas to an old man in a wheelchair.

"Dumb old Grandpa!" the girl cries.

There's a knock at the door, and the mother answers. A man in a three-piece suit hands her a pamphlet and says, "Oldies got you down? Don't wait! Apply today at one of your local dump-off facilities."

She glances at the pamphlet and nods with astonishment. The next scene shows the family at Disney World. They're smiling and laughing and they're all eating Mickey Mouse ice cream bars.

The girl says, "Life is so much better without Grandpa."

"You said it, honey," replies the mother. "Now, how about another ride on Space Mountain?"

Arica looks away from the TV in disgust.

The lobby doors slide open again. An orderly half-drags, half-carries an old man into the building. The orderly has the guy subdued in a full nelson, but the oldie kicks and thrashes about while babbling incoherently. A nurse rushes over with a syringe containing a cloudy mixture.

"Don't make this hard," the nurse says. She aims for the old man's neck but stabs him in the cheek instead. The man's face twists as the bitter sedative shoots down his throat. The nurse curses and grabs another pre-loaded syringe from her pocket. This time, she gets the needle right in the jugular. The man goes limp.

Eloise finishes with the receptionist and turns back to the group. "Would you all like a tour of the facility?"

Julie claps excitedly. "Oh yes, please, show us everything."

"This is our cursing wing," Eloise says as she leads them down a hallway. Faded orange wallpaper peels in several places. Moldy ceiling tiles sag under the weight of brackish water.

"Oh, that's right," Julie says. "I heard you specialize in handling curses."

Eloise beams. "Indeed, we do. Most of our residents can only cast your garden variety bad luck spells, but a few are rather adept with their hexes. We have a fellow who can make your eyeballs two feet wide. Another one can transform lunchmeat into cotton candy."

Toby pauses and licks his lips. "Are we in danger here?"

Eloise says, "Goodness, no, sweetheart." She leans in closer. "We hardly ever have an incident."

Toby frowns.

Eloise tilts her head. "Say, I remember you. You're the grandson of that poor lady who disappeared from here. Your parents showed me a picture of you. You've grown, but I'd recognize those eyes anywhere. Same as hers."

"I... who?" Toby stammers.

"Your granny, Bessie," Eloise says. "Such a shame."

Arica gapes at Toby. "You never told me this was the same place your parents took your granny."

Toby rubs the back of his neck. Everyone's eyes are on him.

"Or that she went missing," Arica says.

"I didn't know my parents dumped her here. I never asked."

"You didn't know where your granny was? How could you send her cards?"

Toby stares at her blankly. "They make cards for oldies?"

"Excuse me," Earnest says. "If it's not too much trouble, I'd like to ask a question."

Eloise looks at him as if addressing a swatting insect. "Very well, Dave."

"How did someone go missing?"

Eloise clucks her tongue. "She must have just walked out on her own with no one noticing." Eloise uses two fingers to mime a person walking. "But don't worry, we have security cameras now to prevent that sort of thing from happening again. It's been six months since she vanished, and we haven't had another incident since."

Arica knits her brow, looks up at the expensive-looking cameras. Does anyone actually watch the feeds? Toby just slides his hands into his pockets and tries to make himself invisible.

Eloise continues, "Here at Withered Oaks, we put security first." She low-fives herself behind her back for saying that with a straight-face, can't wait to watch herself on the security footage later.

The group steps aside to allow two men wheeling a gurney with a zipped-up body bag to pass.

Arica looks at the body bag, then asks Eloise, "What happened to him?"

Eloise sniffs. "Just an oldie who died of appendicitis. He's being taken to our organ extraction team. They'll put his innards on ice for transport to Saint Mary's. A few people on transplant lists are about to get the best phone call of their lives."

"Isn't appendicitis treatable?"

Eloise narrows her eyes. Arica must have failed her class in utilitarian ethics. "Did you hear the part about transplants?"

Arica recoils but says nothing.

"Now, shall we continue the tour?"

"Just take me to my room," Earnest says.

Eloise shrugs. "Demon summoning wing, it is."

Eloise leads them through a maze of identical corridors. To Earnest, it looks like it would be easy to get absorbed by this place and forgotten forever. Eloise might as well be herding him to his execution.

"So, Dave," Eloise says. "How about you tell me more about this demon you summoned?"

"How about I get naked, and you give me a sponge bath?"

Julie smacks Earnest on the back of his head. She will not tolerate backtalk from an oldie. "What he means," Julie says, "is that the incident occurred during a neighborhood barbecue I hosted. All of my friends were there with their kids. The children just were playing, not bothering anyone."

"The little bastards were bothering me," Earnest says.

"Shut it, Dad! As I was saying, the children were just minding their own business. A water balloon fight broke out, and one of the balloons accidentally struck my father in the chest."

Earnest rolls his eyes. He knows they hit him on purpose. What Julie says is such horseshit.

"My, my," Eloise says. "That must have been quite upsetting for you, Dave."

Toby sees Arica's shoulders tighten up. He also sees another excuse to make physical contact. He puts a hand on her shoulder and gives it a squeeze, but Arica slaps his hand away.

"Oh, he was livid," Julie says. "He summoned a demon from my petunia garden."

"You keep demons in your petunia garden?" Eloise asks.

"No, I mean he raised one using my petunia garden."

"Oh, I see." She wags a finger at Earnest. "Such a naughty one, aren't you?"

Earnest glowers at her.

Julie says, "It was made of mud and had two of my favorite yellow petunias for eyes. Before I or any of the other parents could react, the foul creature grabbed hold of two innocent children and shoved their faces inside its abdomen. The coroner later found that the kids' stomachs and lungs had been completely stuffed with mud."

"That's terrible," Eloise says.

Julie shivers. "You have no idea. I was so embarrassed. I thought we might have to move."

"And your daughter could have been hurt."

"Right, that too."

They reach an unoccupied room and Eloise shows them inside. Earnest has to duck his head under the doorway. There is a narrow hospital bed and a particleboard nightstand. A cubbyhole stands in place of a closet. The lack of other furnishings makes the bed a bleak focal point. A drab flower mural adorns the wall, like the kind you might find in a cheap pediatric dentist's office. Arica's shoulders sag at the sight of it.

"Where am I supposed to sit?" Earnest asks.

"Why, on the bed, of course," Eloise says.

Arica sees the remaining light fade from Earnest's eyes. Eloise also notices, but to her, it's a beautiful sunset.

"So, what do you think of your new home?" Julie asks Earnest, not really caring.

Earnest drops his bag on the floor. "I think it looks like the kind of place where hope comes to die."

Arica runs her fingers across her neck scar. She needs to get out of this room. She turns to her mom and asks, "Can Toby and I go exploring while you finish up here?"

"Of course, dear. Just don't bother any of the nurses."

Arica grabs Toby and starts to drag him out of the room. Earnest puts an arm in front of them. "Please," he whispers. "Don't leave me here."

Arica opens her mouth, but nothing comes out.

Julie brushes Earnest's arm out of the way. "It's time to face reality, Dad. You had a good run, but it's over now."

Arica avoids her grandpa's gaze. She gives a half-smile and tiptoes out of the room. Toby shrugs, gives the others a look that says, *what can you do?* He turns and follows her.

"I think we can forgo the rest of the tour," Julie says to Eloise. "You have a rebate check for me?"

"Absolutely. I need you to fill out a few more items, and then I'll hand over your official Receipt of Dumping. If you'll follow me?"

Julie nods and turns toward the door.

"Goodbye to you too," Earnest says.

Julie flips him off behind her back as she follows Eloise out of the room.

Earnest stands there clenching his fists for a hot minute, then takes a deep breath to release his tension. He slumps down on the end of the bed. It crunches in response to his weight. He stares at the mural until tears blur his vision.

Chapter Three

Toby notices Arica working her jaw. "Are you feeling okay?" he asks her.

Arica rolls her eyes so hard they almost fall out of her head. "Sure, Toby, I'm doing splendidly. What could I possibly have to feel bad about?"

Toby flinches. He knows he asked a stupid question, but he doesn't know what else to say.

"Idiot," she mutters.

They're walking down a hallway, heads bobbing left and right, on the lookout for anything interesting. "This place doesn't seem so bad," Toby says as he walks around a large carpet stain. "I bet they even have a gym where your grandpa can get some exercise. Let's look for it."

Arica sighs, but agrees. What else are they going to do? If Withered Oaks has a nice place to exercise, it might make her feel an ounce better about the place. They ask a nurse where the gym is, and he happily points them in the right direction.

"Aren't you curious about what happened to your granny?" Arica asks Toby.

He sticks out his bottom lip. *These things happen.*

"If my grandpa is going to stay here, I want to make sure this place is safe."

"My granny went crazy and killed an entire family. It's other people I'd be worried about. Who knows who she might hurt running around loose?"

"You think she's dangerous?"

"Totally. She had these wicked telekinetic powers. This one time, she tossed a minivan 200 feet in the air and let it crash to the ground. There was a family of four inside. The city didn't feel like spending the money to extricate their crushed bodies from the twisted debris, so they dug a giant grave and dumped the whole wreck inside."

"That's messed up," Arica says.

"The police said my granny was confused and didn't know what she was doing. A few days later, my parents dumped her off."

"Well, something would have happened by now if she escaped. Maybe Eloise killed her and covered it up."

"You're suspicious of everyone."

They spy a set of wide double doors at the end of the hall. It looks like someone finger-painted the word "Gym" onto the doors.

"That's because people are selfish and want to control you," Arica says.

"I don't want to control you."

Arica shakes her head. Toby does want to control her. He's just more subtle about it. "Thank you for always being honest," she says.

Toby nods. Praise from Arica is better than any drug.

They reach the entrance to the gym and shove the doors open. They only make it a few feet inside before Arica stops dead. What she sees convinces her she has to rescue her grandpa from this place, no matter the cost.

In the telekinetic wing, Wilford the milkman enters the room of a resident and sets a crate of milk on the floor. Wilford looks around the room at the dull, yellow walls, the window caked with dead insects, and the cracked, unwashed linoleum. A rough, raggedy recliner sits in an alcove on the back wall. Why is it even here? None of the sad souls in this place ever receive visitors. Near the recliner, a mini fridge hums. Its door is green and slightly corroded. Wilford glances at the emaciated form occupying the bed. The man is asleep, and Wilford is determined he stay that way.

Wilford leans his head into the hallway, looks both ways, then ducks back inside and shuts the door.

"Looks like it's just you and me, chief."

Wilford kneels and selects a milk bottle from the crate—his special bottle. Instead of milk, it contains propofol, a substance that looks like milk but is actually a powerful anesthetic.

Wilford smiles as he grabs a dirty syringe from his pocket and removes the cap. He jams the needle into the bottle and withdraws 100 ml of the drug. He replaces the bottle, then steps over to the sleeping man. With practiced skill, Wilford inserts the needle into a paper-thin vein on the man's right forearm and injects the contents. After replacing the cap, Wilford pockets the needle and steps to the foot of the bed. He slides his hands underneath the mattress, grabs the edges of the tucked sheet, and pulls it up and over to reveal the man's feet.

Spasms of ecstasy rock Wilford's body as he gazes upon the man's gnarled toenails. They are thick and brownish-yellow from years of untreated fungal infection.

"Wilford, my man, you have hit the jackpot."

Before he was hired as a milkman, Wilford had to settle for tracking down vagrants and hoping their nails would be suitable for his purpose. But all that is in the past. Now, he has access to a plethora of neglected oldies and their overgrown, diseased nails.

Wilford removes the needle-nose pliers from his other pocket and grips the edge of one of the man's discolored nails. With one clean motion, he rips the nail right off the nail bed. It makes a sound like an onion getting peeled. He holds the nail up to the light. "This will do quite nicely."

He places the nail under his nose and inhales the burning, putrid aroma. "Oh, such fragrance. How blessed am I?"

He wraps the bloody nail in a tissue and pockets it, then repeats the process for the remaining nails. Afterward, Wilford replaces the frayed sheet and tucks it under the mattress. He could have treated the oldie's now bleeding toes, but Wilford is more concerned with moving product than cleaning up after himself.

Before he leaves the room, he places two jars of milk inside the man's mini fridge.

The gym holds the same vile stench as the rest of the building, with the added aroma of soiled clothing and unwashed bodies. There are treadmills, exercise bikes, ellipticals, and rowing machines. Directly in front of Arica and Toby are a dozen bikes lined up in a row, each with an oldie peddling furiously. Heavy cables run from each of the bikes to a series of car batteries perched on equipment racks. Monitors fastened to the racks display power output in kilowatt-hours.

Arica's eyes water. "They're using the residents to generate electricity."

"Of course we are," a voice says.

Arica and Toby turn to their left and see one of the orderlies—a broad-shouldered, cheerful fellow with a twinkle in his eyes that says this is the best job in the world.

"They get to feel useful, and we get to offset our utility costs," the man says. He turns and zaps the closest rider with a cattle prod. "Faster, you loggerhead!" He turns back to them and says, "Please excuse me. You can't take your eyes off of them for a second."

Toby looks at Arica as the man walks away. "Well, this should put your mind at ease."

"Are you kidding me?"

"Not only can your grandpa stay in shape, he'll be giving back to the community. It sure beats him just sitting around, sucking up oxygen."

Arica shakes her head. "These people don't have a choice." She gestures to the thick shackles securing the residents to their machines.

Toby turns up his palms. "They're basically children and need to be told what to do. Life has come full circle."

"I just don't understand why they put up with it. With their collective powers, they could stage a revolt."

Toby shrugs. "Why don't you ask one of them?"

There's a group of seniors on treadmills in the back row that aren't currently under surveillance. Arica marches right up to one of them, with Toby scurrying behind. Now that they're closer, they can see that the treads are made of sandpaper. There's a lady covered in sweat who's chained to the treadmill in front of Arica. She has bloody scrapes on her knees and shins from prior falls.

"Excuse me," Arica says. "Can I ask you something?"

The woman doesn't react. She just throws one foot in front of the other, trying to keep pace. They think the woman might not be able to hear Arica's scratchy voice, so Toby repeats the question. The woman turns her head toward them but looks past them.

Arica asks, "Why do you let the staff treat you like this? Why not fight back?"

The woman tries to wipe sweat from her brow but she can't reach it because of the shackles. She gives her head a few shakes instead. "It wouldn't do any good," she whispers. "Despite the propaganda, most people here aren't that powerful." She pauses to gasp for air. "If anyone does act up, they get sedated and punished."

Arica raises an eyebrow. What would this woman consider punishment if being chained to a treadmill is normal?

"I'm not strong enough to resist, anyway," the woman continues.

Arica sighs, deflated.

"But there is one among us who might help."

Arica asks who, but an orderly approaches, and the woman clams up.

"Let's get out of here," Toby pleads. "I don't want to get in trouble for disturbing the natives."

Arica clutches her turtleneck. "You go on ahead. Tell my mom I want to say goodbye to my grandpa before we leave."

Earnest is lying on his bed, staring at the cracking ceiling when Arica walks in. The bed is much too short, so his feet dangle off the end.

"Come to bid me farewell?" he asks.

"I didn't want to leave without saying goodbye."

"Your mom will be glad I'm gone."

"I won't be."

"She'll finally have her house back. Now she can invite guys over without me embarrassing her."

Arica chuffs. "Today she's meeting some guy she found on a hookup site. I doubt it will turn out any better than the last one."

Earnest swings his legs over the edge and sits up. "That's because your mother bangs anyone with a pulse."

Arica gasps. "What? How can you say that?"

"I can say it because it's true. It's not like I raised her that way. She was a good kid... *at first*. Then she started running around with God knows who doing God knows what. When she met your father, I hoped she would settle down. But I guess he saw her for what she truly is—a selfish piece of trash with loose morals."

"Grandpa!" Arica cries as she takes a step back.

Earnest grins. He forgot how good it feels to insult loved ones.

"It's not fair to judge other people's sex lives," Arica says. "And don't think I forgot about the time I caught you watching the neighbors having sex. 'I like to watch' is not a valid excuse. You're sick and you need help."

"I need help? What about you, little missy? You're the one who's tried to kill herself what, two times now? They should lock you up, not me."

It's actually four times. No one knows about the time Arica tried to disembowel herself with a bread knife. She passed out before she could cut deep enough. Then there was the incident with the roadkill. Her penchant for attempting suicide started when her father left. If her own dad didn't want her, Arica thinks, she must not be worth much.

Arica shuffles her feet. "I'm better now. Toby has helped."

"Oh, I bet he has. If you're not careful, you're going to end up just like your mom."

"It's not like that," Arica says. "And I'm nothing like my mom."

"If you say so, you leg-spreading delinquent. Also, your voice sounds like you've been smoking for half a century."

"At least I didn't summon a demon that murdered children!"

When she sees the hurt on her grandpa's face, she knows she went too far. She's about to apologize when Earnest orders her to get out. She throws up her arms and leaves, and Earnest lies back down and resumes staring at the ceiling.

Chapter Four

Arica storms down the hallway, mouth dry and stomach tight. Earnest has no right to speak to her that way. Maybe her mother is right, and Arica should be glad they dumped him. It's not Arica's fault that he's grown old and dangerous. When older relatives develop powers, that's basically it for them. They no longer have a place in civilized society. And actually, if they have any decency, they just off themselves like Arica tried to do. They should realize they're not wanted.

Arica silently berates herself. She can't start thinking like her mom.

With a start, Arica realizes she's lost. All the corridors look the same. Other than the occasional fake plants and the faux wooden handrails running the length of the halls, there are no decorations. Occasionally, she sees signs of life: an errant wheelchair or battered oxygen tank. Someone left a crash cart in the middle of the floor, the paddles dangling. Arica wonders if it was successful on whomever it was last used.

The stink is overwhelming. It smells of burning feces and ripe garbage, thick enough to coat her throat and invade her pores, threatening to engulf her senses. She wants to sterilize her clothes as soon as she gets home, but she's not allowed to touch the bleach anymore. No matter, she'll just burn her clothes instead.

She wipes the sweat from her brow with a shaky hand. *Why is it so hot?* Her tongue sticks to the roof of her mouth, and her leg muscles tense. The stagnant air feels like a thick layer of mud on her exposed skin. It sticks to her arms, legs, and face. The walls close in, the floor unsteady. Withered Oaks feels like a living entity that will devour her soul if she does not escape immediately. Arica searches frantically for an exit, having no desire to join the doomed souls already consumed by this blight on humanity.

She is about to yell for a nurse when she hears music coming from up ahead, crackly and tinny. She creeps along the hallway, seeking the source of the chilling tune.

The hallway opens into a community room. Stark oak tables take up most of the floorspace. The chairs are bolted to the floor. There are gaps between a few of the seats where wheelchairs can fit. A listless old man plays solitaire at the far table. A carnival lamp perched on the corner of the table shines down like a spotlight on cards he barely has the strength to lift.

"Excuse me," Arica croaks as she approaches the man. "I need you to tell me where the exit is."

The man ignores her. Just continues dealing himself cards. He has only three cards left, so the same king of diamonds appears over and over.

"Dude, you've lost. Might want to start a new game."

But he doesn't want to start a new game. This one is endlessly entertaining. He keeps turning over the same stack of cards.

"Look, are you going to help me or not?"

Arica decides the old man is too far gone to even notice her presence. "Fine. Just sit there and rot." She turns to go.

His raspy voice says, "Mr. Fuzzles will curse you!"

Arica spins back around. "The hell you just say?"

But the man just flips his cards, cloudy eyes peering out from half-closed lids.

Arica shakes her head. She has no idea who Mr. Fuzzles is, nor does she care to find out.

"I hate this place." She turns and pushes on.

The music gets louder, the odor worse. Her stomach roils and her head spins. She grips the handrail to steady herself. At the end of the hallway stands a scuffed metal door that's slightly ajar. She stumbles her way toward it, her breath coming in shallow gasps. The room beyond is the source of the eerie music. It sounds like something depressed oldies would listen to. Shrieking violin strings so sharp it makes her teeth ache.

Arica sticks her head inside the room. She squints as she struggles to understand what she's seeing. An old woman strapped to a bed. A tube sock stuffed in her mouth. Three figures in pale-yellow hooded bathrobes standing over her. A gramophone hissing and popping in the corner. Only one face is visible—an old man with disturbingly large eyeballs. They're at least a foot in diameter and are attached to the man's eye sockets by thin optic nerves that look like they will rip apart any second. Red veins spiderweb the pus-encrusted eyes. Massive corneas reflect the flickering light of nearby candles.

Eyeball Guy grips a long metal skewer with a marshmallow affixed to the end. As Arica watches, the man holds the marshmallow over one of the flames until it's a nice golden brown. Then, he turns to another robed figure who is holding two graham crackers, one of which is smeared with chocolate. Eyeball Guy sticks the marshmallow onto one of the crackers, then the other man puts the two halves together and hands the newly formed s'more back to Eyeball Guy. He gazes at the woman and removes the sock from her mouth.

"Please—" is all she gets out before Eyeball Guy shoves the s'more into her mouth, followed again by the sock. Then he takes the skewer, still with marshmallow debris on the end, and slowly inserts it into the woman's nose. She writhes and bucks against her restraints while the sock muffles her shrieks. Eyeball guy pushes the skewer through tissue and cartilage until it pierces the brain.

Arica lets out a throaty scream and jerks her head back. She spins on her heels and takes off back the way she came. She flies through the community room at a dead sprint. The man who was playing cards is gone. The cards now form a tower that almost reaches the ceiling. Like miniature Stonehenges stacked on top of each other.

She rounds a couple corners and speeds past two orderlies that pay her no mind. She sucks down great quantities of fetid air while her heart threatens to explode from her chest. Off to her left, she spies an empty resident room. She ducks inside and slams the door behind her.

Arica, gasping for breath with her back against the door: "What the hell was that?"

She runs over to a window and fumbles with the latch. She pulls the window open, scurries through, and shuts it behind her.

She's in a vegetable garden. Tall tomato vines line both sides of a dirt path. She navigates around the edge of one of the vines and comes across rows of cabbage and artichoke. There are also raspberry bushes, oddly out of place among the vegetables. The garden is enclosed with a ten-foot chain link fence with gnarly razor wire running along the top.

An old man in a tank top and running shorts steps into view. He has as much hair on his chest as he does coming out of his ears. He smiles at Arica, revealing coffee-stained dentures caked with rotting food particles. Even from several feet away, Arica smells his putrid breath. She doubles over and vomits on an artichoke.

The man grins. He's found a broken wing to mend. "You had a little accident," he says. "Don't worry, I'll take care of it."

He knocks his head back and opens his mouth. There's a sickening crack as his jaw comes unhinged. His saggy cheeks stretch as he opens his pie hole wide enough to insert a bowling ball.

Arica laughs despite herself. This is hardly the strangest thing she has seen today.

The man produces a tremendous sucking force from his gaping maw, pulling Arica's soupy vomit and the artichoke off the ground and into his mouth. He gulps them down greedily. Arica dry heaves, then stumbles over to the fence and grabs hold, shaking it violently. "Someone let me out of this goddamn freak show!"

"Awe, don't fret," the man says as he swallows the last of the delicious goop. "Let Daddy Suckface help you."

Daddy Suckface glances up at where the barbed wire meets the brick wall. He opens wide again and commences the sucking process. The wire pops off the corner of the fence, twangs through the air and whip-slashes a bird in a flight, sending it careening into the dirt. The end of the wire reaches Suckface's mouth, and he takes it in with much gusto. Arica rushes to the edge of the fence and starts climbing.

Daddy Suckface draws the wire down his throat, tearing and slicing flesh along the way. It gashes his stomach and continues into his small intestine. Suckface coughs up blood as the wire lacerates his bowels.

Arica makes it to the other side of the fence as the wire makes it to the other end of Daddy Suckface. He grabs hold of the wire and alternates pulling from each end like he's flossing the inside of his body. This is the most fun he's had since the time he swallowed a family of porcupines.

Chapter Five

"What happened to you back there?" Toby asks Arica for the third time.

Arica crosses her arms. "Nothing happened. I told you I'm fine. Now, will you please drop it?"

After escaping the garden, Arica ran around the building until she found the parking lot. Her mother wanted to know what had taken so long, but Arica rebuffed her. She's still processing everything that happened and doesn't know who she can trust. Plus, she knows her mother would just accuse her of spouting lies. Julie doesn't want anything to mess up her day.

Each year after dumping their oldies, the neighborhood attends the After Dump Celebratory Clambake. It's a chance for everyone to cut loose and rejoice in their freedom from being saddled with old people.

Julie pulls into the parking lot where the festival is being held and finds a space. "Time for you kids to put on your biggest smiles."

Arica scowls as they climb out of the car. Toby bites his lip and bounces on his feet. He's anticipated this event ever since he learned that Arica's grandpa was getting dumped. This is a thrilling opportunity to spend quality time with her. He fantasizes about winning a giant teddy bear at one of the booths. He'll give it to Arica and she'll fall in love with him.

The park is buzzing with festivities. Laughing children with funnel cakes and reams of cotton candy chase and shove each other. People carry helium balloons or bags of recently won goldfish. A booth sells t-shirts with screen prints of happy families waving goodbye to their oldies. There are patrols of police officers armed with tranquilizer guns. They wear ceremonial jackets made from the sewn-together bones of rebellious oldies.

"Feel free to look around," Julie says. "But I want you at the lunch table in thirty minutes. Those clams aren't going to shuck themselves."

"We wouldn't want to miss that," Arica says without a hint of sarcasm.

Once she and Toby are out of earshot, Arica finally fills him in on Daddy Suckface and the barbed wire. She leaves out the part about the woman who received a s'more lobotomy, just in case Toby's granny met with a similar fate.

"That is so messed up," Toby says. "But it shows how dangerous and crazy oldies are. It would just be a matter of time before your grandpa killed someone else with his demonic energies."

"I guess," Arica says. But she knows that whatever is happening at Withered Oaks involves more than just caring for magic-casting dementia patients.

They come across a dunking booth with a short line.

"Oh, I want to play dunk-the-oldie!" Toby says. Arica considers dragging Toby away, but gets in line with him. Many families have old people that didn't make this year's cut, either because they aren't demented enough or their magic abilities haven't sufficiently developed yet. Fortunately, these oldies can still serve the community by acting as comic relief.

A woman in her eighties with liver spots is being forcibly helped back onto the seat above the tank. She is soaking wet and complaining about her artificial hip. The woman's nephew shushes her as he and another man succeed in placing her back on the perch. It is a chilly, blustery day, and the tank water is dense with ice.

The booth operator hands three baseballs to the next kid in line, but he misses the target with all of his shots. Finally, it's Toby's turn. He whoops as he hands the booth operator a dollar and receives the baseballs in return. The old lady suspended above the tank hugs her midsection and shivers.

"Can I g. . . g. . . go home now? I'm. . . so cold," she says through chattering dentures.

"Shut your hole, auntie," her nephew says. "If you keep complaining, I'm not giving you your heart pills today."

"Be careful, Toby," Arica says.

But Toby is already unloading with his first shot. It clips the edge of the target with a *twang* but isn't enough to trigger a dunk. His second shot is dead-on. The seat collapses, plunging the old lady into the frigid tank. She flails and splashes. The cold water burns her skin. She tries to stand, but her foot slips and she twists her ankle. She tries to cry out but gags on the freezing water.

"Booyah!" Toby cries. He turns to high-five Arica, but she leaves him hanging. Toby shrugs and collects his prize—a stuffed plesiosaur.

The dunked oldie struggles to reach the edge of the tank with her bad ankle. She flounders about, choking on the icy water. Her nephew frowns. He looks at Toby and gestures toward the tank. "Hey, do you mind giving me a hand?"

"Sure thing." They both know the booth would have to shut down if the oldie drowns. Toby hands the plesiosaur to Arica and strides over to the side of the tank. He and the nephew reach out and each grabs hold of an arm. They pull the woman up and over the edge. She flips upside down and slams to the ground, the force of the impact dislodging some of the water in her lungs. The nephew thanks Toby and then he and Arica go on their way.

"Why do you have to be such an asshole?" Arica asks as she shoves the plesiosaur back into Toby's arms.

Toby flushes. Not because he thinks he did anything wrong, but because Arica is unhappy with him.

"What do you mean?" he asks. "I was just trying to help."

"Yeah, sure you were. I saw the bloodlust in your eyes when you were hurling those baseballs. You enjoyed every second of it."

"Uh, yeah, I enjoyed it. Why wouldn't I?" He sucks his cheeks in. "Don't you think you're being a little dramatic? Having fun is the whole point of being here."

They stop in front of a booth giving away free novelty tubes of salve for gum pain. Arica and Toby each grab a tube as they continue arguing.

Arica says, "It shouldn't be at the expense of other people."

"They're barely even people anymore."

"They still deserve respect."

Toby clutches the plesiosaur with sweaty hands. "What matters is whether the oldies can respect themselves. I couldn't respect myself if I didn't play the role society expected of me."

"You're such a mama's boy," Arica fumes.

"Just because you hate your mom doesn't mean I have to."

A woman leading a small child by the hand approaches them and says, "Will you please keep it down? There are families here."

Arica glares at Toby. It was obviously his voice that was carrying. No one can hear Arica beyond a few feet. She smiles at the woman and then storms off. Toby follows, just like Arica knew he would.

Toby feels he should apologize, but he can't think of the right words. Instead, he opts for distraction. He catches up with Arica and asks, "Why don't we check out the bouncy castle?"

Arica pauses for a moment. She has fond memories of playing in a bouncy castle when she was younger. It might be fun to relive them again.

"Okay," she says. "But this isn't over."

"Got it."

Knowing which direction to go is easy. They just have to follow the screams and laughter. But when they reach the castle, Toby realizes he has made a grievous error.

Children are jumping around inside as usual, but apparently the festival's organizers figured out a way to incorporate the bouncy castle into the reason for the holiday. Inside the castle, an oldie is trapped in a ring of children. The kids are jumping in unison, the oldie being tossed up and down like a rag doll. The old man thrashes about in a hopeless attempt to control his momentum. Arica and Toby can hear the man's brittle bones snapping like dried twigs. It horrifies Arica that none of the adults standing around are doing anything to stop this. Instead, they cheer on their crotch fruit while watching the mayhem unfold.

"Stop this!" Arica cries.

Only a couple of the parents are close enough to hear her, but they don't acknowledge her. Arica runs up to the castle and kicks off her shoes.

Toby's butterflies return. He runs over to her. "Hold on. What are you doing?"

Arica ignores him and marches up the inflated ramp. A yellow-shirted supervisor shoots his arm out to block her way. "Whoa," the man says. "You're not allowed in there. You're way too old."

Arica laughs at the hypocrisy. She goes back down the ramp and turns to face the man directly.

"Move along now," he says.

Instead of moving along, Arica stares him down.

Toby says, "Come on, Arica. Let's go." But she isn't listening. Arica takes another step towards the man. Without warning, she bends her knees, springs up and strikes his chin with the heel of her palm. The savage blow snaps his head back and sends his teeth crashing together. Eyes roll into the back of his head as he crumples into a heap.

"Holy shit!" Toby cries as he drops the plesiosaur.

Arica leaps back onto the ramp and rushes into the castle. The closest kid to her is a chubby boy with chapped lips. Arica grabs him around the waist, twists her body and tosses the kid out the entrance. There are audible gasps from the parents as the boy bounces off the ramp and spills onto the dirt.

Arica's next targets are three kids clustered to the left of the battered old man. She barrels into them, tackling all three at once. She makes it to her feet just as a little girl comes running toward her, thinking this is a new kind of game. Arica disabuses her of this notion by kicking her in the stomach, launching her backward. An older boy takes issue with this and bares his teeth, charging. Arica sidesteps and the boy slams into the netting. Arica catches him on the rebound, lifts him up and suplexes him. Within moments, the children are stumbling toward the exit, many of them in tears.

"There's more where that came from, you worthless brats!" Arica calls after them. She turns to attend to the old man. He's finally come to a rest. One of his legs is bent at an unnatural angle. He draws in on himself, trying to shrink from the world. Arica kneels over him.

"Are you okay, sir? Try not to move. I'll get you some—"

The man cranes his swollen neck and spits in Arica's face.

"Ugh." She backs away as she wipes the spittle with her sleeve.

The man's eyes are full of angry tears. "I don't need your help."

"Let's go!" Toby calls out. Arica turns and sees him on the other side of the castle. He found an alternate exit concealed in the rear netting and is holding it open for her.

"We have to go, now!" he cries, glancing left and right frantically.

At first, Arica thinks Toby is being a drama queen. But a quick survey of the scene reveals angry parents pointing and shouting at her. A few are scrambling over each other to get up the ramp. Arica runs for the rear exit, drops and slides through.

"Here," Toby says as he hands over her shoes. She slips them on, then she and Toby duck behind a tight row of tents.

Chapter Six

Toby holds Arica's hand as he leads her over thick electrical cabling and around weather-beaten wooden crates. Arica feels too exhilarated over having beaten up those kids to mind the physical contact. But that ends as soon as they find themselves back in the throngs of people.

"Thanks for grabbing my shoes," she says as she takes her hand back.

"No problem," Toby says. "We might want to get out of here before they throw us out." He glances around nervously.

"Screw those elder-abusing fascist dirtbags. They can come after me if they want. Now, where the hell are those clams?"

Toby points toward the center of the park. "I think they're back that way."

They don't make it far before they encounter a crying child—one that Arica has nothing to do with. He's standing near a large booth that houses another carnival game. There is a row of children seated at the front, each of them armed with a swivel-mounted dart gun. Their target is on the other end of the booth—an old man strapped to a vertical, rotating wooden disk. There are darts embedded in both the wood and the man's tired flesh. The rotation causes the blood around his puncture wounds to form up like pepperoni.

Arica walks up to the boy and kneels. "What's wrong, kid? Is that your grandpa up on the wheel?"

The boy shakes his head. "No," he says between sobs. "But I couldn't hit him with the darts and now I'm out of money, so I can't try again." The boy notices an errant dart stuck in the dirt and yanks it out with his little hand.

Arica narrows her eyes and clenches her teeth.

The boy continues, "Can I please have some money so I can shoot the oldie?"

"You most certainly cannot." She snatches the dart out of the kid's hand and storms off, ignoring his protests. Toby hurries to catch up with her.

"Whoa, what are you doing?" he asks.

"Just wait here. I'll be right back."

But Toby doesn't want to just wait right here. Toby wants to feel useful. He defines himself to the degree to which he is helping others. Well, mainly Arica. He tails her as she weaves her way back between the tents toward the bouncy castle.

When Arica nears the castle, she crouches low in case there are any irate parents still in the vicinity. She sighs when she sees Toby sneaking up behind her. Without acknowledging him, she slinks up to the back of the castle. As Toby watches in horror, Arica jams the dart into the thick vinyl. She rips the dart out, then stabs the castle several more times. Air rushes out of the punctures, but it's not fast enough for her. She tries to use the dart like a knife to gouge a wider opening.

Toby cringes at this display of vandalism. He's normally inclined to follow the law, but he's also inclined to follow Arica. He decides that if he breaks the law, too, maybe Arica will see him as hip and edgy and like him more.

"Here, let me try," he says.

He takes the dart from Arica and jabs it near a cluster of holes she's already made. Gripping the dart with both hands, he jerks it through the material, opening up a four-inch gash. The air rushes out so fast it feels like a leaf blower.

They duck back through the tents, ditching the dart along the way. Once they reenter the crowds, they pause and look at each other, gasping for breath.

"That was so awesome," Arica says. "Those malicious parents and their grubby kids can get their kicks somewhere else."

Toby likes the way her eyes sparkle with mischief. He takes a long breath. "I have to say, I admire the way you stand up for your beliefs. Even if they are a tad misguided."

She scowls at him. "Let's eat."

Dozens of tables covered with gingham cloths are lined up in parallel rows. Large buckets overflowing with ice and raw clams sit at regular intervals. Each bucket contains a small wooden mallet. There are also pots containing cooked clams, carrots, onions, and corn. Fortunately, Julie saved seats at the end of one of the last rows. Arica hopes it's unlikely anyone will spot her there.

She and Toby sit down next to Julie, who is conversing with a man on the opposite side. He has close-cropped black hair held in place with a generous amount of product. The man's teeth are blinding white. Dark stubble covers his chiseled jawline. He tilts his head when he laughs in a way that says *I like you. Isn't this fun?* If there exists a secret club of men who specialize in crashing clambakes, Arica is sure he's a member.

"And that's when I got slapped with my third DUI," the man says

Julie laughs at what is apparently the end of a funny anecdote. "You're hilarious," she says, then looks at Arica. "Isn't he, darling?"

Arica raises an eyebrow.

"This is my daughter, Arica, and her friend, Toby," Julie says to the man.

"Pleasure to meet you both," he says. Arica forgets his name as soon as he gives it. Marvin? Mark?

"Help yourself to some clams," Marvin or Mark says as he gestures to the bucket in front of them. He grabs a few of the clams and lays the sweating mollusks on his plate. Arica and Toby each grab a couple as well. Arica wonders where the clams come from. They are nowhere near an ocean.

Julie gazes lovingly at the man and says, "The kids and I are having such a good time today."

"Is that what we're doing?" Arica says.

"Well, isn't that lovely?" the man says.

Julie winks at him. "We're so thrilled to have dumped off my father this morning."

"Congratulations!" He wedges the edge of his knife inside a clam. "I know that must be an enormous relief."

"Oh God, yes. I feel so bad for those families whose oldies didn't make the cut. They must be so disappointed."

The man nods his head sympathetically. "I can't imagine having to go another year pureeing peas for my worthless nana. Sometimes I just gave her baby food, but that stuff's not cheap, you know." He finishes prying open the shell.

"You poor thing." Julie reaches across the table and touches his arm.

He grins. "Fortunately, a spot opened up at Village of the Bygones, so I folded up Nana in a plastic storage bin and Fedexed her overnight."

"What the hell is wrong with you?" Arica cries.

The man looks genuinely confused by the question.

"Arica," Julie warns, "you'll mind your manners if you know what's good for you."

"No, it's okay," the man says. He looks at Arica. "I appreciate your concern for my financial well-being, but my rebate check was never in doubt. I included an oxygen tank so she wouldn't arrive dead."

Julie says, "That was sweet of you. Please excuse my callous daughter."

He laughs it off. "No worries. Which scrapheap did you dispose of your dad on?"

"A place called Withered Oaks. Heard of it?"

The man goes quiet for a beat as he stares off into the distance. He wipes his mouth with a napkin and wads it up. "That's interesting. I've heard some weird stories about that place."

"Like what?" Arica asks, sitting up straight.

The man clears his throat dramatically. "Well, first of all, Withered Oaks wasn't the first nursing home built on that land. The original facility burned to the ground before you were born. It was the oldest nursing home in the county. That location was chosen for an odd reason. Supposedly, oldies would wander there naturally once they started developing powers. It was like they were drawn to it. I guess people figured it made sense to build a home there."

"How do you know all this?" Arica asks.

"I work part-time for a historical preservation society. Most of my days are spent poring through old records and piecing together a narrative. I also interview anyone willing to talk."

Toby finally speaks up. "Have you heard anything about people going missing?"

"Only rumors. Nothing concrete. Mostly what I've heard is that the home seems to be popular among professional musicians. I also bartend for orchestras, and I often hear Withered Oaks come up in conversation. Not sure about the context."

"That's odd," Julie says. "The staff didn't say anything about musical performances when they went over the entertainment options."

"They also have unusually tight security there," the man continues. "High fences with razor wire and security cameras. I understand wanting to keep the oldies from escaping, but normally a moat filled with starving alligators is enough to do the trick."

Arica wonders how Earnest is making out. She figures he feels like one of those depressed dogs she always sees in commercials for the animal shelter. The ones whose owners abandoned them. They sit on cold concrete floors in dirty cages, wondering why their families don't love them anymore.

Julie says, "Whatever the deal is with Withered Oaks, I'm sure my dad is where he belongs." She raises her bottled water. "Cheers!"

The man returns the gesture. "I feel like I'm where I belong, too." He flashes her his winningest smile. Julie blushes while Arica curls her lip. He picks up another clam, cracks it partway open, then holds it vertically in front of his mouth. He gives Julie bedroom eyes as he slips his tongue inside. He works his slug-like flapper up and down, then in soft circles around the tender meat. Then he places his lips on the clam, slurps hard, and gulps down the juicy prize. Julie moans involuntarily while Arica vomits in her mouth.

Toby scrolls on his phone, trying to think of an excuse to extricate himself from the horrors unfolding in front of him. Then he notices two of the tranquilizer police approaching from behind. He puts his hand on Arica's leg to draw her attention to them.

Shit. Arica's first instinct is to play it cool, but it only takes her a second to dismiss that in favor of her second instinct—to fight.

With a shriek, Arica grabs the bucket of clams and hurls them over her shoulder, followed by the bucket itself. Most of the mollusks and ice cubes strike the officer on the right, while the bucket crashes into the other officer's chest, ricocheting off his bone jacket and sending him stumbling backward.

"What the hell are you doing?" Julie screeches at her daughter.

Arica grabs the edge of the table, twists, and throws her legs over the bench. She lets go with her left hand and uses her right to launch herself forward. The officer on the left is so startled that he fires his gun reflexively. The dart whizzes past Arica and nails Toby in the ribcage. His eyelids flutter as he slumps over.

Arica tackles the officer on the right and they tumble to the ground, the tranquilizer rifle pinned between them.

"Stop this madness!" Julie yells while clutching her hair. "You're ruining our clambake!"

The guy she's been flirting with does nothing to intervene. The spectacle is too entertaining for him.

The officer struggles with Arica despite her being half his size. He isn't used to encountering resistance, as he normally targets oldies for harassment.

Arica gets her hands on his face and is about to gouge his eyes out when his partner grabs her by her hair and tosses her to the side. Arica recovers, charges again, but the officer on the ground lifts his rifle and pulls the trigger. The dart pierces Arica below her collarbone. The excruciating pain mercifully only lasts a second before the drugs kick in and short-circuit her brain.

Chapter Seven

As the late afternoon sun sinks toward the horizon, Earnest is still lying in bed, mind churning. His entire family abandoned him just to get a fat rebate check from the government. He supposes he shouldn't have been so hard on his granddaughter, but it's not as though she stuck up for him. Arica had the chance to protest when her mother first announced her plans for Earnest's forced relocation, but she chose silence.

Earnest is too depressed to eat, but he's not about to give his new lab-coated overlords an excuse to shove a feeding tube down his throat. If he could turn bitterness into fuel, he'd be all set, but sadly he still requires organic sustenance.

He wills his stiff frame to get out of bed, bones creaking. He gets dressed and walks to the cafeteria to see what he can stomach. The place is grimy and smells of despair. The chalkboard menu offers chicken cacciatore and stuffed peppers, the latter with a line crossing it off. Why didn't they just erase it once they ran out? Maybe they want you to know what you missed out on. *Better luck next time, assholes.*

He passes on the remaining entrée, opting only for a side of buttered baby carrots. He takes his tray and shuffles past the tables as he just wants to eat in his room in peace. But a voice from one of the tables calls out to him.

"Hey, new guy. Come over here."

Earnest grimaces but makes his way to the table. A man with eyes the size of basketballs smiles at him. The man's eye sockets are normal-sized, so his massive eyeballs protrude out in front of his face. Earnest can't figure out how the man's optic nerves can support so much weight.

"I'm Rick," the man says. "But my friends call me Cornelius because of my massive corneas." He lets out a chuckle.

Earnest shakes Cornelius' hand and introduces himself. There are two other men seated at the table. One has tumors all over his body that are excreting some kind of purple liquid. Cornelius identifies him as Pierre. The other guy is covered in blurry, faded tattoos. He has long, wispy hair dyed black. He says his name is Snapdragon.

"Pull up a chair," Cornelius says.

"No thanks," Earnest says. "I'm pretty tired, so I'm just going back to my room."

"Suit yourself," Snapdragon says. "But you ain't gonna survive in here without friends."

While Earnest already thinks of Withered Oaks as a kind of prison, now he wonders if he needs to join a gang and file his toothbrush into a shiv. He shakes off the thought and forces himself to look into Cornelius' eyes. "Did the eyeball guy I heard about curse you?"

Cornelius laughs. "We don't curse each other here without the other person's permission. No, I'm the eyeball guy."

"You did this to yourself?"

"Sure did. It's how I relieve boredom. Plus, it gives me amazing eyesight. Watch this."

As Earnest watches, the man's eyes increase in size to over three feet in diameter. The massive sclerae smoosh together. They droop so low that they are now resting on his food tray.

Pierre doesn't acknowledge anything that's happening. He's hunched over, picking at a slice of apple pie while his tumors ooze purple droplets onto the plate.

"Impressive," Earnest says, gazing at the unnaturally large eyeballs. "You'll have to tell me how you do that someday. Now, if you'll excuse me, it's been a long day." He turns to leave.

"Have a good night," Cornelius says.

They watch Earnest go. "That dude seriously needs some meat," Snapdragon says. "His bones look like they're gonna tear through his skin any second."

Wilford pulls the shades on the lone window in his efficiency apartment. The carpet gives off a musty scent courtesy of a leaky air conditioner the landlord won't bother fixing. The wood paneling is bubbled and warped. A single lightbulb casts a dull yellow glow.

Wilford sits at his bench. He opens a pouch, holds it upside down and shakes until all the toenails have tumbled out. He takes a magnifying glass and inspects each one, occasionally using a razor blade to shave off bits of keratin. His only goal is to slightly improve their appearance. He leaves most of the diseased build-ups intact, just like his clientele prefer.

Wilford deals in providing black-market toenails to professional musicians in the world's finest orchestras. The wind players covet diseased toenails because they make the best reeds. Playing with a toenail reed is quite illegal, but they provide such a rich and velvety sound that musicians pay top dollar for them. And Wilford needs all the money he can get to survive what's coming. He doesn't know exactly what it is, but he hears enough whispers at Withered Oaks to make him nervous. Contrary to popular belief, most of the oldies are not senile. And when people with magical abilities talk, Wilford is smart enough to listen.

If he knew for sure what was coming, he could at least try to stop it. However, his desire to maintain the status quo isn't entirely selfish. Sure, he loves money, but he also enjoys a society where his tax dollars go toward the construction of roads and bridges instead of greedy oldies sucking down social security. Some argue it's actually more expensive to house oldies in special nursing homes instead of leaving them be, but those morons don't know what the hell they're talking about.

Wilford counts the number of decent nails he has. "Just won't do," he mutters. He needs at least eight or nine more to fill his most recent orders. He'll have to go back to Withered Oaks tonight when he has more freedom to work. Fortunately, they gave him a key, so he can come and go as he pleases. If anyone asks, he'll just pretend he's getting an early start on tomorrow's milk deliveries.

Back in his room, Earnest sets his tray down on the crappy nightstand next to the bed. Having no chair, he slumps down on the edge of the mattress. In this light, he sees how mushy and unattractive the carrots really are. They are moist and pale, like armpits. Earnest grabs the tray and heaves it across the room where it clatters against the bathroom door. The rejected root vegetables stick to the laminate floor.

Earnest studies the carrots, his rage building. As he watches, they start moving. They scoot along the tile, their shapes undulating like fat inchworms. They leave trails of buttery juice in their wake. A few of them meander listlessly. Others lift their little carrot worm heads as if sniffing the air.

Earnest thinks of how little gratitude Julie shows him for raising her. How she takes his love and support and spits on him. How she leaves him for dead as soon as things get inconvenient.

The carrots alter course and head for each other. They each have their preferred method of locomotion. Some ripple like millipedes, others flip and flop about, and a few take to rolling.

The first two carrots meet. Their squishy bodies smoosh themselves together to form a worm carrot twice the size. The other carrots join up, fashioning themselves into a giant carrot mass that pulses and quivers and heaves. Its body becomes segmented and tapered like a scorpion. It sprouts tiny legs and a tail. There isn't enough carrot matter left over to form claws or a stinger, but the creature is reluctant to start over and shape itself into something different, so it decides to go without.

Earnest looks upon the carrot demon with a mixture of excitement and disgust. The thrill of righteous anger made incarnate is intoxicating, yet this demon business is a sordid thing. Plus, this latest creation doesn't exactly look capable of carrying out a murderous revenge plot.

"What the hell am I even supposed to do with you?" Earnest asks. "You look as menacing as a hemorrhoid."

Sensing his master's displeasure, the carrot demon scurries under the bed. Earnest is considering how to dispose of it when a man bursts into his room.

"Hey, can you help me?" the man asks. "I'm not supposed to be here."

Earnest laughs. "Who the hell is?"

The man gives him a blank look. He looks twenty years old, yet he's wearing clothes that went out of style eons ago. It was as if he raided his great-grandfather's closet. He has a stick-on nametag that reads *Milton* in magic marker.

"Why did you oldies bring me here?" Milton asks. "I'm supposed to be at work." He grabs his hair and rocks back and forth on his heels, crackling with nervous energy.

"Where's work?" Earnest asks.

"The Adult Megaplex on Q Street."

Earnest vaguely remembers a porn shop in the old downtown that went out of business when he was a kid. A new elementary school was built nearby, so the city forced the smut shop to shut down. This had gravely disappointed Earnest because they had sported a huge voyeurism collection that he treasured.

"Well, I'm sure they can do without you for a few hours," Earnest says.

"Do without me?" Milton dry washes his hands. "Do you have any idea how irritated customers get when they can't find exactly what they're looking for? No one wants to just hang out in our store. They want to grab and go. If they can't find their favorite Brazilian deep throats because they're mixed in with barely legal stepsisters, it's my ass."

The carrot demon pokes its grotesque head out from under the bed near where Milton stands.

"You're way too young to get stressed out like this," Earnest says. "Take some advice. Figure out what really matters in life before it's too late and you end up like me."

The carrot demon grows an arm and sprouts a tiny orange knife. It plunges the blade over and over into Milton's ankle, but he doesn't feel anything because the blade is too flaccid to do any damage.

Milton's eyes water and he swallows hard. Then he furrows his brow as confusion takes over. He looks at Earnest as if seeing him for the first time. "Hey, can you help me?"

Earnest squints at him. "I think we've been over this."

Milton twists his mouth. His eyes dart left and right. "What the hell is this place? Did you kidnap me?"

Whatever Milton's problem is, Earnest decides it's way above his pay grade. Of course, everything is above his pay grade because he doesn't have a job. No one wants to hire old people.

"Yes, I kidnapped you," Earnest says.

Milton visibly relaxes, his shoulders drop.

"I sought revenge for all my overdue late fees," Earnest says. "But today's your lucky day, because I'm letting you go. If you step out into the hallway and find a person in a white uniform, they'll escort you out."

"That's more like it," Milton says. "I'm the forgiving sort, so why don't we just chalk this up to you being a confused oldie? No need for me to press charges."

Earnest puts a hand over his heart. "That's incredibly kind of you."

Milton's smile says *I know it is*, but also *watch yourself, old man*.

As soon as Milton is gone, Earnest stoops and yanks the carrot demon out from under the bed. He holds it at eye level and inspects it more closely.

"Anybody in there?" Earnest asks it. "Are you really a demon, or maybe some form of living rage?"

It's anyone's guess what these manifestations actually are. Some believe they're demons, others think they're projections of the oldie who summons them. Like a poltergeist in physical form. Others think they're interdimensional beings that feed on long-held grudges.

The creature's only response is to squirm as it tries to free itself from its maker's hands.

Earnest carries it into the bathroom. The bathtub has a door on the side to allow for easier access. Earnest feels a moment of pride that he isn't that infirm yet.

He tosses the creature into the tub, then strips down and climbs in. He turns the showerhead on full blast and twists the temperature dial until it's fully in the red. He angles the scalding hot water downward, where the carrot demon will receive the brunt of it. It squeals and gurgles as parts of its carrot flesh melt away. Desperate to escape, it tries to scurry up the side of the tub but can't find a grip. Then it scuttles toward Earnest, looking for mercy, but he just kicks it back under the jets.

"Die, you pathetic waste of space."

Earnest jams his heel into the creature, splitting it in half. The scorching water burns his leg, but Earnest is long past caring.

"Useless! Worthless!"

He stomps and stomps until the demon is nothing but a puddle of mushy fiber. Earnest kicks all the bits down the drain, slams the faucet closed. He collapses into the fetal position and weeps.

Chapter Eight

After the grogginess from the darts wore off, the police released Arica and Toby to Julie. She was so furious that she dropped them off at Toby's without saying a word, which is fine with Arica. She doesn't particularly want to be around her mother right now.

Now, Arica sits cross-legged on the floor in Toby's bedroom, playing with a loose strand of carpet. She wraps it around her finger. Like most of the carpet in Toby's house, it's crusted with dried blood.

Toby leans against his chest of drawers, watching her. He hates that they got in trouble with the law. They were told that because they had no prior record, they would be let off with a warning. But if there are any further incidents, the next stop is reform school. Toby regrets having to leave the festival so early. He was really looking forward to eating popcorn while watching oldies knife each other in the gladiatorial games.

"Good thing they let us go," Toby says, trying to make conversation.

"Whatever," Arica says. "You should have helped me. There were only two of them."

Toby scoffs. "I was unconscious, remember?"

Arica shakes her head. She knows the truth is that Toby isn't sure what he would have done if he hadn't been shot right away.

"Are you angry with me?" he asks sheepishly.

"No, but I need to know I can count on you."

He looks her in the eye. "I promise you can."

"Okay then. Make sure you show it next time."

Toby relaxes a bit. She's still going to be his friend.

More silence passes and Toby fidgets with a knob on one of the drawers. He wishes he knew what to say to make Arica feel better. His brain is empty and useless. They should be having a good time, not ruminating over the dumping of her grandpa. It's like getting upset over graduating to a new grade level. Dumping oldies is a natural part of life.

"Got a splinter up your pee hole?" Arica asks, noting the scowl on Toby's face.

He slumps against the dresser. "I just don't enjoy seeing you depressed."

Arica lets the carpet fibers unwind from her fingers and brushes off a few of the dried blood flakes. "You should have seen him," she says. "He was so upset. I'm pretty sure he hates me now."

"I doubt that. Deep down, he knows where he belongs."

Instead of smacking Toby across the face like the little bitch he is, Arica says, "He belongs at home with me and my mom."

Toby perks up as an idea occurs to him. "Hey, how about if I give you your birthday present now?"

"My birthday is two weeks away."

Toby drops his eyes.

"You really got me something?" Arica asks, tilting her head.

"Of course I did." He goes to his closet and retrieves a gift bag. It has a yellow metallic shimmer meant to imitate gold. Fancy ribbon adds flare to the handles.

"Here you go," he says as he hands it to her. "It looks like gold because that's what you're worth your weight in."

She cringes at the lameness of that comment but thanks him anyway. She removes the tissue paper from the bag as Toby takes a seat beside her on the floor. She pulls out what looks like a binder, then realizes it is a photo album. She opens it and flips through the glossy pages. They are filled with pictures she and Toby have taken of themselves throughout their lives. Birthdays, hiking adventures, trips to the mall, all there.

After Arica's father left, she fell into a deep depression. Her moodiness exacerbated her already tenuous friendships. But Toby always stuck by her.

She turns to Toby and puts a hand on her chest. "Thank you." She looks back at the photos. "You were always there for me when I needed you."

"And I always will be." He puts an arm around her.

"I'm glad you said that, because I'm about to need you again."

Before Toby can reply, they hear *splat... splat... splat...* coming from the hallway. It sounds like someone is walking barefoot through puddles.

Arica and Toby turn their attention to the open doorway just as Mary, Toby's little sister, appears. She is covered in blood. It drips from her ears, pours from her eyes, and spurts out her tiny nose.

"Hey, Mary," Toby says. "You can come in."

When she opens her mouth to thank him, half a pint of blood spills out. A small bucket she wears around her neck catches some of it.

Mary's blood is cursed. It has been ever since she refused a hug from a random oldie in a park. The man had dementia and didn't take kindly to Mary rebuffing him. Because of the curse, Mary's blood lost the ability to coagulate. It leaks from every orifice. However, she also replenishes her blood at the same rate she loses it.

Mary doesn't have any friends her age. They are all too freaked out to be around her. They think she has some disease they might catch. One day, Mary found Toby's Super Soaker in the garage. She filled it with her blood and ran around the neighborhood, spraying the other kids. It was the most fun she's ever had, even though she was grounded after several angry parents complained.

Not everyone shares this fear. There are weirdos who think Mary is blessed. Touched by an angel. They think Mary's blood holds the secret to eternal life. Fountain of youth in human form. They want to rub her blood on their bodies, paint symbols on their walls, and drink it straight. So, what did Mary's parents do? They started bottling and selling her blood. Buy three, get one half off. They make so much extra money that they can afford to take luxurious vacations. They never take Mary with them, of course. That would be too inconvenient, even if they hired a nanny. No, they need their little money maker to stay home and fill bottles from the bucket around her neck. And because Mary has to stay, Toby also has to stay to babysit. But he never complains.

"Check out what your brother got me," Arica says. She rotates the album so Mary can see.

"I know," Mary says as she walks over. "It's all he's talked about for weeks." She sounds exasperated in an endearing sort of way. Mary hasn't let her condition or her isolation beat her down. Arica also spends a ton of time alone, although her avoidance of people is by choice.

Mary sits down in front of them and looks over the pictures, careful not to drip any blood on them. Whenever she sees a photo with her in it, she bounces a little.

"What did you mean a second ago?" Toby asks Arica. "You said something about needing my help."

Arica is quiet for a moment, then she fixes Toby with a steely gaze. "We're going back in. Tonight."

"Back where?"

Arica says nothing. The *where* is obvious.

"But they're closed now. No visitors after dark." Even as he speaks, Toby's stomach flutters as he senses where the conversation is heading.

"I didn't say we were going in the front door."

"Are you gonna break in?" Mary asks. "I wanna come."

Toby knows the look on Arica's face. She will not be dissuaded. "What do you want to do? Break a window?"

"Won't have to. We can get in the same way I escaped earlier, through the garden."

"This is so cool," Mary says.

"No, it's not cool," Toby protests. He gets up and starts pacing. "Our parents will kill us. Mine will, at least. Especially after what happened today."

Arica stands and says, "We'll wait until tonight when they're asleep, then we'll take my mom's car. She'll either be passed out drunk or off banging that weirdo from the clambake."

"My daddy says your mommy's a drunken whore," Mary says, eager to demonstrate her knowledge to the older kids.

"Shut up, Mary!" Toby cries.

Arica kneels in front of Mary and wipes some of the blood dripping from her eyes. "Your daddy doesn't know everything. Mine sure didn't." She gets up and looks at Toby. "Are you with me?"

Toby clenches his jaw. He loathes the idea of getting into trouble again. But he's also afraid Arica won't like him anymore if he says no. "Why can't we just go tomorrow?"

"Because my grandpa might not have that long. I don't want whatever happened to your granny to happen to him." Arica also doesn't want him to get tortured to death like that poor lady she saw. "We need to find out what's up with that place."

Toby sighs and stares at the floor. Arica smiles because she knows she's already won.

Chapter Nine

After Earnest applies a generous amount of ointment to the shower burns on his legs and feet, he thinks back to his encounter with Cornelius and his buddies. Was he too abrupt with them? Snapdragon is probably right. Earnest should make friends. At least then he might not be as miserable.

And that's how he finds himself in the cursing wing. He isn't sure which room belongs to Cornelius, and he doesn't feel like asking anyone. After a search of the bottom floor, Cornelius is nowhere to be found. Earnest heads to the second floor. He passes by a room with a wastebasket parked outside that is overflowing with bloody rags. A quick peek inside the room reveals a few staff members overseeing a patient who is just out of view. Earnest thinks he hears one of them address the man as Mr. Suckface, but decides he must be mistaken.

A dismal lounge interrupts the procession of patient rooms. Here the hallway widens into a space that includes a sad, fraying couch with multiple biological stains. Two women with matching floral print dresses are seated on the couch. They are watching an old game show on an ancient, dusty television with a partially washed-out screen.

To the right of the TV is a third woman trapped in a wooden pillory, head and hands bound by the device. She wears a bright orange bathrobe. Her cheeks are puffy and her forehead sags over her eyes. She shifts her weight back and forth, trying to relieve some of the pain in her hunched-over spine. The two women on the couch ignore her, absorbed in their game show.

Earnest places himself in front of the couch and the TV. He looks back and forth between the women seated there and the one stuck in the pillory.

"Excuse me," he says to the women. "What the hell is this about?" He gestures to the trapped woman.

The women ignore Earnest, leaning to their sides to see around him.

Earnest steps away from the couch and inspects the pillory. It's a heavy oak contraption, sanded down and covered in clear lacquer. A comically oversized steel padlock holds the clasp in place.

"Hello? Ma'am? Are you okay?"

The woman doesn't respond, and Earnest can't tell if she's even acknowledging his presence because he can't see her eyes. He glances down at her bare feet and notices her toenails are missing. He turns back toward the women on the couch.

"Would one of you mind explaining what is going on here?"

One of the women glances up at him. She raises a shaky index finger to her mouth in a shushing gesture. Then she reaches inside her mouth, rips out her dentures, and flings them at Earnest. He sidesteps, and the dentures go flying past him, smacking the pilloried woman right in the face. She is oblivious to this newest affront. Some of the denture spittle makes it into Earnest's mouth and nose, and he wretches in response. It tastes like baby food. For a cat. So, kitten food.

His heart sinks into a black hole of despair as he contemplates spending the rest of his life with these wackadoodles. He considers going straight back to his room, but the desire to talk with someone about what he's seen wins out.

Earnest searches the opposite side of the wing until he finally locates Cornelius' room. He knocks on the open door and Cornelius waves him inside. Earnest is relieved to find that Cornelius' eyeballs are mostly back inside his head, though they are still abnormally large. His room is bigger than Earnest's and includes a table in the corner. Snapdragon and Pierre are there as well, seated in the same positions they had in the cafeteria. It's as if a giant scooped them up and transplanted them here without interrupting their conversation. There is a Scrabble board on the table, but no tiles have been placed.

Earnest takes the open seat, crosses his arms and looks at Pierre and Snapdragon. "So, Cornelius here is the eyeball guy. What about you two?"

Snapdragon snaps his fingers and a small fireball erupts in front of him before dissipating just as fast. "I can curse the air and set it on fire. Technically, I'm listed as an elemental, but really, it's just another form of cursing. Shit's all connected, man."

Earnest nods as if this makes sense, then looks at Pierre. "And you?"

Pierre glances at Earnest, then at Cornelius.

"Pierre had a stroke and has trouble speaking," Cornelius says. "But when he hit the ripe old age of seventy, he developed the ability to curse people's legs and crack their femur bones."

Snapdragon snorts. "Yeah, the only problem is whenever he uses his power, a disgusting-ass wart tumor thing sprouts from his body and drips weird shit everywhere."

Pierre drops his head in embarrassment.

"What about you?" Cornelius asks Earnest. "Why did your family decide you'd be better off in our company?"

"I summoned a demon that killed two children."

"A demon? Shit," Snapdragon says. "That wasn't no demon."

Earnest looks at him askance. "What do you know of it?"

"I mean, it was sort of a demon. No one can actually summon a demon in the flesh. They always take the form of something already existing."

Earnest considers this. It's as good a theory as any, and might explain the incident with the carrots.

"What was your entity made of?" Cornelius asks Earnest.

"Mud and flowers," Earnest says.

Cornelius nods appreciatively. "Mud would be a good demon component. Nice and malleable."

"I know what I did was wrong," Earnest says. "But my daughter was already looking for an excuse to get rid of me. She says I have dementia, which is bullshit."

Snapdragon smirks at Cornelius. "This one catches on quick."

"Not everyone here is sick," Cornelius clarifies to Earnest. "And you're supposed to be both mentally ill and magic-inclined before you get sent to a place like this."

Snapdragon pounds the table with his fist. Scrabble tiles go flying. "It ain't right, what they're doing."

"Young people," Cornelius says. "Our own family members. They just cast us aside like rotting fruit."

Earnest nods. When he was younger, he supported dumping oldies. He dumped his own father at a similar facility, then promptly forgot about him. It's just the way things are done. But now that he's on the other side of it, Earnest is having second thoughts.

Milton springs into the room and says, "Hey, can you guys help me? I'm not supposed to be here."

Earnest rotates in his seat and regards the interloper. Milton doesn't recognize him.

"Hey, Milton," Cornelius says.

"How do you know my name?"

Cornelius stands and points to Milton's chest. "It's on your nametag."

A bewildered Milton glances at his nametag and squints. Cornelius steps out from behind the table, walks over to

Milton and puts a hand on his shoulder. "There's been a gas leak," Cornelius says. "It's affecting our memories. Here, let me take you to where you'll be safe."

Cornelius escorts Milton out of the room. Earnest looks at Snapdragon for an explanation.

"Milton ages in reverse," Snapdragon says. "Poor bastard is technically 150 years old or some shit."

Earnest whistles. "That explains a lot."

"The shitty part is that he knows nothing past what he learned at his current age. I think his body is, like, twenty now."

Pierre says something, but his words are so slurred that Earnest can't make them out.

"Fuckin' right," Snapdragon says. "I'd kill myself too if I could remember long enough to get the job done."

Cornelius returns and reclaims his seat. He explains, "We make him wear a nametag, so he's slightly less freaked out when he discovers we already know his name. I hear it wasn't so bad back when he first arrived, but he doesn't even remember coming here. There's a poster on the wall in his room that explains the situation, but sometimes he wanders out and forgets everything."

"When that happens, we rotate the explanations we give him," Snapdragon says. "The gas leak is a classic. Sometimes we tell him he was in a major car accident that scrambled his brains. Other times, we act just as confused as he is."

Pierre mumbles something.

"That shit is sadistic," Snapdragon says, but laughs anyway.

Earnest jams a bony finger in his ear, digging for wax. "There's something else I wanted to ask." He withdraws his finger and inspects his prize. "I saw a woman trapped in a pillory. What's that about?"

Cornelius darkens. "That's Maven. She got caught stealing ice cream again."

"Ice cream?" Earnest asks as he wipes his finger on his pants.

"Shit's so stupid," Snapdragon says. "Ice cream is the only thing that makes her happy. Why not just give her as much as she wants? I'll tell you why—because they want us to suffer. Makes us easier to control. It's all about power, man. They have it and we don't. They chain us up like dogs until they've broken our will."

"But why does stealing ice cream warrant torture?"

Cornelius says, "Administrator Eloise thinks public humiliation is a really keen idea. It's never worked, but that doesn't stop her from trying."

"What about Maven's feet? It looked like her toenails had been removed."

Snapdragon says, "She had to have done it to herself. People around here sometimes go nuts and rip out their damn nails. How else would you explain it?"

"We believe it's some kind of stress-induced mass hysteria," Cornelius adds.

Earnest wonders if every retirement home is as messed up as Withered Oaks, or if he just drew the short stick.

"They'll let her go in the morning," Pierre says. Earnest is getting better at understanding him.

Earnest asks, "I heard someone's granny got dumped here and then went missing. How is something like that even possible?"

Cornelius raises an eyebrow. "You'd be surprised how long it takes staff to realize when someone is gone."

From the hallway, a nurse says, "Lights out in fifteen minutes, gentlemen."

"Yes, ma'am!" Snapdragon calls out. Then, under his breath: "Fuckin' bitch." He lights a tiny fireball with his anger, then closes a fist around it, smothering the flame.

Earnest shifts in his seat. "I guess I need to say goodnight. I feel like I have no control over my destiny anymore. I'm at the mercy of people who are decades younger than me."

Cornelius leans forward and lowers his voice. "What if we told you we knew a way to change all that? A way for us to wrestle back our freewill from these young pricks who think they know everything?"

Snapdragon says, "And a way to teach those bitch-ass little crybabies a lesson they'll never forget?"

"Can you elaborate?" Earnest asks.

Cornelius gives a wry smile, then says, "Some of us are having the same dream. In it, we are visited by Mr. Fuzzles."

"Mr. . . Fuzzles?"

Cornelius nods. "We can't see him, but we can hear his sweet voice. He's our almighty savior—an immensely powerful being who loves us and will soon emerge to lead us to victory over those who would enslave us. Using our combined powers, he will cast the Curse of Ages. It will mark the beginning of a new era."

"And what is the Curse of Ages?"

"We don't know yet," Snapdragon says. "But it's going to be something totally awesome. Like, maybe Mr. Fuzzles will make people's heads fuckin' explode."

"People's heads aren't going to explode," Cornelius says.

"You don't know that, dude."

"If Mr. Fuzzles kills all young people, then there would eventually be no more old people."

"Huh," Snapdragon says.

"Whatever it is," Cornelius says, "it will flip the balance of power in our favor for good."

Earnest considers their words. It sounds like bullshit to him, but any chance at revenge is worth pursuing. "How can I help?"

Chapter Ten

Arica, Toby, and Mary are in the living room finalizing their plans to break into Withered Oaks. Arica had to cajole Toby to let them "borrow" his mother's minivan. "Dude, I'm an excellent driver," Arica says. "I promise, no scratches." Toby buries his concerns deep down so she won't think he doesn't trust her.

"I'll fill up the water bottles and grab some snacks," Toby says.

"I'll get the bolt cutters!" Mary squeals. She scurries off toward the garage, leaving a trail of fresh blood on the crunchy carpet. The fibers beg for mercy as their ability to absorb any more of the girl's fluids has long since been exhausted.

Arica thinks Mary isn't right in the head, but she rubs her turtleneck and wonders if she's really any better.

"I'll get a bag," Arica says. She goes into the bedroom and dumps out Toby's backpack, scattering pens and textbooks.

She returns to the living room to find Mary dragging the bolt cutters down the hall. She's also carrying a Super Soaker that's almost as long as she is. The giant, pill-shaped compartment attached to the barrel has several holes drilled into it from which rubber tubing springs. With Toby's assistance, she attaches the tubes to various parts of herself. A couple of them run up her nose. They tape two others underneath her tear ducts. Another goes to an IV in her neck. With every beat of Mary's tiny heart, cursed blood transfers to the

Super Soaker. Toby knows it isn't good for much other than scaring kids, but Mary wants to feel like she is helping, so he indulges her.

Toby affixes the last of the tubes. "There you go. You're all set."

Arica comes over and inspects the handiwork. "You're a good brother," she says to Toby.

"You really think so?"

"Absolutely. I would choose you as a brother any day."

Toby frowns.

"You can't have him," Mary says defiantly. "He's my brother!"

Arica laughs and strokes Mary's hair. "Don't worry, I would never take him away from you."

Mary gives a wide grin, showing off her bloodstained teeth.

"Now," Arica says, "let's go commit some crimes."

Earnest is back in bed, sleep eluding him. Cornelius and the others gave him a lot to ponder. Whoever this Mr. Fuzzles is, Earnest will follow him if it means exacting vengeance on Julie and all the other ungrateful young people. However, Earnest is dismayed that Cornelius could not explain what this super curse is supposed to be, even though Snapdragon repeatedly assured Earnest it will be *badass*. When Earnest asked how he could help, Cornelius just told him to stand by for further instructions.

Earnest feels like he's being considered for membership into an exclusive club. That's enough to make him feel special for now, but Cornelius needs to include him in something more substantial soon. Earnest loves the idea of being useful and committed to a cause. And if that cause is world domination, so much the better. Earnest thinks that if he were in charge, he would hit young people where they're most vulnerable. He would strip away the smugness they wear like armor, drag them into the light and lay bare their deepest insecurities. He wants them to feel the same humiliation and degradation they force old people to endure.

Earnest has to pee. He tries to throw off the covers, but his arm won't move. At first, he thinks his limb might be trapped under his leg or otherwise asleep, but he tries his other arm and finds it won't respond, either.

Am I having a stroke? He tries to sit up, but his abdominal muscles ignore his brain's commands. His skin grows hot and his pulse accelerates. His mind searches desperately for answers. Is this a medical problem or did someone curse him?

From the hallway, a noise like a table saw winding down. And something soft, like a gurgle. He hears the doorknob turn and the door creak open. Then silence.

Earnest strains to see in the darkness. Thin shafts of weak fluorescence coming from the security lights outside his window do little to help.

Suddenly, a new sound breaks the stillness: *VAROOOOM CHOONK. VAROOOOM CHOONK.*

"Um. . . hello?" Earnest says.

VAROOOOM CHOONK. VAROOOOM CHOONK.

Something substantial is ambling toward him. He can barely make out its blocky form. It's impossible to see detail in the darkness. There is just an impression of sharp angles and hard protrusions.

One last *VAROOOOM CHOONK* and it's standing over Earnest. He tries to yell for a nurse, but his voice fails him. A glint of light reflects off a thin wire approaching his left eyeball. An explosion of white-hot pain as it pricks the cornea and burrows into his eye. His vision blurs with tears and blood. Inside, he howls in agony.

The wire coils around the optic nerve as it makes its way to his brain. Earnest screams for his body to move, but nothing happens. Intense pressure builds in his cranium like he is having an aneurysm. The pain crushes his mind like a star collapsing in on itself.

Just when he thinks his skull will split open and expel his brains to all corners of the room, he mercifully blacks out.

When Earnest finally comes to, he leaps out of bed, smashing on the light switch. He is alone. There is a throbbing ache in his temple and a stabbing pain in his eye. He rushes into the bathroom. After his eyes adjust to the harsh light, he leans toward the mirror, spreads his eyelid, and inspects his violated organ. Ruptured blood vessels cover the sclera, and yellow-orange pus pools at the edges.

Earnest turns pale and draws shallow breaths. What the hell happened to him? It definitely wasn't a dream, given the physical evidence. He turns the faucet on and splashes water in his eye. It helps, but only marginally so. Instead of looking like he tried to perform surgery on himself with an ice pick, it now looks as though he has a nasty infection.

He puts a hand to his skull, trying to soothe his pounding headache. His fear gives way to anger and disgust. His mind grasps for some explanation that might make sense, but his brain is too foggy.

"What if it comes back?" he whispers to himself.

Earnest stumbles out of the bathroom and opens the door leading to the hallway. He sticks his head out and surveys both directions, making sure there are no staff. The hallways are dim, but he detects no movement. He steps out of his room and closes the door behind him. He doesn't know if there is a punishment for being out of your room after curfew, but he sure as hell doesn't want to end up in the pillory.

There is no sign of the creature that attacked him. He creeps along the wall toward the stairwell. The only illumination is a dimmed overhead.

He climbs to the third floor with one hand on the railing and the other on his aching head. When he reaches the exit, he gingerly pushes it open. Like the first floor, there is no activity. He tiptoes along until he reaches the cursing wing. He finds the door he wants and quietly lets himself in. He flips the switch, and the room is bathed in rough, institutional light.

"Wha—" Cornelius murmurs. "Who's there?"

"A guy who just got assaulted in his sleep." Earnest bounds across the room and grabs hold of Cornelius' shoulders and shakes him. "Did you hear what I said? I was attacked."

Cornelius rubs his bulbous eyes. They ache from the intrusive light. "I think I'm the one being attacked."

Earnest's words tumble out of him. "There was someone in my room—a monster. It shoved something in my eye and it hurts like hell. I tried to stop it, but I couldn't move."

"Oh, *that*." Cornelius props himself up by his elbows. "That happens to everybody. It's nothing to worry about." He rolls over, hoping he can fall back asleep quickly.

Earnest grabs Cornelius and pulls him back. "What the hell do you mean? That thing might have laid eggs in my brain."

Cornelius sighs. He resigns himself that he won't be going back to sleep anytime soon. He folds his pillow and places it behind his back so that he's almost sitting up.

"Think of it as an initiation," Cornelius says. "A rite of passage. Most people who come to Withered Oaks are visited at least once."

"At least once?" Earnest says, more alarmed than ever. "You mean it might come back?"

"If you're lucky. Only the most promising among us get multiple visits."

"What does that mean—most promising? And what the heck is it?"

"We call it the Emissary," Cornelius says. "We believe it to be an agent of Mr. Fuzzles."

"Mr. Fuzzles," Earnest repeats. "Our mystery savior who will free us of our bonds?"

Cornelius nods. "He sent forth the Emissary to find who among us is most worthy of serving him."

"By stabbing wires into our brains?"

"Consider yourself fortunate. Pierre got a partial lobotomy. Screwed up his speech center. But it will all be worth it in the end, I assure you. He tells me great things."

Earnest does not feel assured. "How do these. . . experiments determine our worthiness?"

Cornelius shrugs. "It is not for us to question Mr. Fuzzles."

"Did Mr. Fuzzles tell you he sent this Emissary in one of your dreams?"

"No," Cornelius admits. "But what else could its function possibly be?"

Earnest paces the room. This still isn't making sense to him.

"I know this all must be quite confusing," Cornelius says. "But you have to trust me."

"I thought you said Pierre has trouble speaking because he had a stroke."

"I regret lying to you. I needed to know I could trust you. The fact the Emissary chose you is all the proof I need that you're on our side."

We'll see, Earnest thinks.

"Not everyone here believes in our mission," Cornelius continues.

"I'm assuming that includes the staff?"

Cornelius smirks. "The staff don't even know our mission exists. And they think the Emissary is a myth conjured up by senile old fools looking for attention."

Earnest would be inclined to believe the staff if he hadn't experienced the Emissary himself. There is something undeniably strange going on at Withered Oaks, and although his experiences frighten him, he also feels an undercurrent of excitement. If he can harness that and fuse it with his desire for revenge, it might be enough to keep him going.

"I am with you," Earnest says.

Cornelius takes Earnest's hand in his. "Excellent, friend. With the help of Mr. Fuzzles, we will make families across the globe pay for what they've done. The proverbial lake of fire will melt the flesh from their bones and damn their souls for all eternity to ceaseless agony and unimaginable suffering."

Chapter Eleven

Arica kills the minivan's headlights as they approach Withered Oaks. Thin beams of moonlight push their way through a patchwork of clouds, branches, and leaves. The world is cast in black and gray and silver, a landscape of rocks and trees without detail. Her foot on the brake pedal, the engine rumbling at idle speed, she scans the area, finding a spot where gravel lines the side of the road. She pulls over, tires crunching softly. She, Toby, and Mary climb out of the car, Toby with the backpack and Mary with the Super Soaker. Toby flinches as an owl hoots in the distance.

Arica directs them to crouch low behind a row of spruce trees. They are still a few hundred yards out and are in no danger of being spotted, but Arica is new to this stealth invasion business and is determined to go all-in.

"Are you sure you want to do this?" Toby whispers to Arica. "It's not too late to call this whole thing off."

Arica sneers at him. "If you want to run home and hide under your bed, then be my guest. Mary and I are staying. We have a job to do."

Mary looks up at Arica and gives a determined nod. She's on board. Her blood bucket sloshes faintly, and somehow reassuringly.

Toby swallows, wants to slink back into the shadows. Even Mary is against him. He wishes he could just fast forward through the night and know that everything is going to be okay. Tomorrow, things will go back to normal, and he'll make sure that Arica never has a reason to be mad at him ever again.

Earnest is finally drifting off to sleep when Cornelius shakes him awake. At first, Earnest thinks he's being attacked by the creature again. He opens his mouth to scream, but Cornelius covers it with his hand.

"Shh. . . It's me, friend," Cornelius says.

Earnest's expression goes from shock to confusion.

Cornelius removes his hand from Earnest's mouth. "Our lord and savior, Mr. Fuzzles, is calling us to glory. The time has come to execute the Curse of Ages!"

Earnest is nonplussed. "But I left your room maybe thirty minutes ago. How can it be happening already?"

"I don't know, but isn't it great? We all heard the call in our dreams. Surely you heard it, too?"

"I haven't fallen back asleep yet," Earnest says as Cornelius drags him out of bed. Earnest notices that Cornelius is wearing a baby blue bathrobe with a hood sewn on. He takes another robe he has bundled under his arm and shoves it at Earnest. "Here, put this on." Cornelius makes for the door.

"Wait, where are we even going?"

"You'll see."

"Do your thing, Toby," Arica says.

They are standing in front of the wrought iron gate that bars the way to Withered Oaks, secured with a menacing chain. Toby hesitates, then reluctantly removes the bolt cutters from his bag, hands shaking. He looks over at Arica and half-grins. He swallows hard, then steps up to the heavy chain. He targets a link and pushes the two handles of the bolt cutters together, but nothing happens. He shoves them together harder, but still, nothing happens. His face flushes as he imagines Arica's disapproval of his physical weakness. He inches closer to gain more leverage, then slams the handles together with all his might, grunting loudly. Just as he fears his veins will burst with the effort, the bolt cutters slice through the link. He turns and grins at Arica as if to say, *Did you see that?*

Arica says, "Yeah, real impressive. Now, get that chain off and let's go."

A visibly pained Toby pulls off the chain and drags it to the side of the gate. Not waiting for him, Arica pushes the gate open and heads up the driveway, with Mary scampering along behind her.

As they approach the compound, they see the outline of Wilford's van.

"What the hell is the milkman doing here?" Toby asks.

"How should I know?" Arica says.

"Sometimes I get up for milk in the middle of the night," Mary says.

"Shut up, Mary," Toby says.

"Don't be a pickle prick," Arica says to Toby.

"What's a pickle prick?" Mary asks.

"It's what your brother is, apparently."

Mary giggles while Toby's face burns. He knows he shouldn't unleash his irritation on Mary, but he wanted to lash out and Mary is a convenient target. And a much safer one. Why risk upsetting Arica further?

"The milkman being here doesn't change anything," Arica says. "I doubt we'll run into him. We're just going to have a look around. Maybe copy some documents or break into their computers."

Toby wonders if Arica knows anything about breaking into computers. It also occurs to him that there should still be nurses on duty. "Isn't there also a night shift we'll have to avoid?"

Arica silently curses herself for not considering that, but she has too much pride to admit the mistake. Plus, she's the leader of this group and leaders always know what to do.

"I thought of that," she lies. "Trust me, it won't be a problem. This place is enormous. There are plenty of places we can hide."

Arica's tone says that there will be no further protests allowed. They squeeze up against the building, then Arica and Toby get on their hands and knees. They crawl along the side of the wall, keeping well below the windows. Mary also crouches low. She's not tall enough for anyone to see her from a window, but she wants to imitate her brother. She holds the Super Soaker out in front, the occasional drop of blood falling from the barrel. They round the corner and continue crawling until they reach the garden fence. Arica doesn't want to risk having Mary try to climb it, so they cut a hole with the bolt cutters.

The garden is deserted, as it should be at this late hour. They reach the window Arica escaped from earlier. The latch is still undone, so she slides the window open and peaks inside. Dark. Quiet. Same pungent odor. It reminds Arica of the time she found a dead raccoon flattened in the middle of the road. She peeled off the skin and ate the raw stringy meat, hoping she would contract an illness that would kill her. The only thing it did was keep her glued to the toilet for an entire day. Withered Oaks smells just like the results of her folly.

Arica scrambles through the opening and beckons Toby and Mary inside. Mary dumps out her blood bucket. Toby gives her a boost and then climbs through himself.

Arica whispers, "Let's look for a records room first."

Toby is still skeptical of Arica's plan, but he has to admit this is exciting. Now that they've sneaked inside undetected, much of his dread has evaporated. For the first time in a while, he feels everything will work out just fine.

Eloise watches her security monitors with growing bemusement. "Just what in the world are these kids trying to accomplish?" The fools triggered a perimeter alarm before they had even made it past the main gate.

Eloise is also monitoring several residents donning ridiculous pastel robes modified with hoods and trying to be discreet about it. She knows that many of them are involved in some kind of weird cult, but it's nothing more than a pathetic attempt to feel like their lives have purpose. Their only real purpose now is to stay out of the way of the young. And to entertain her. Eloise had few sources of entertainment as a child. Her father drowned in a kayaking accident, then her mother took a job overseas, so she was raised by her grandfather. He was a mean, nasty old man who resented having to spend his golden years raising yet another kid, and he let Eloise know it.

He never let Eloise watch TV or play with toys. One time, Eloise found an electronics kit at a garage sale. She kept it hidden under her bed, waiting for her grandfather to go to sleep. Then she would take it out and learn all about circuits and capacitors and diodes. She was a natural, rarely needing to look at the instruction manual. She eventually figured out how to convert the kit into a radio, but it squawked so loud that it woke up her grandfather. He made her watch while he smashed the kit with a 2x4. Then he turned it on her backside. He told her it was her fault her mom left, because Eloise was a pathetic child no parent could ever be proud of. Eloise loathed listening to her friends chat incessantly about their happy lives and all the cool things they got to do—concerts and parties and trips out of town. And the lack of beatings.

Now, Eloise has all the theater she could ask for. She rarely goes home anymore, choosing instead to sleep on the leather couch in her office so she doesn't miss any of the oldies' antics. If they ever bore her, Eloise creates entertainment in other fun ways. Sometimes she directs the staff to serve an oldie food she knows they're allergic to. During winter, she shuts off the heat at random intervals, forcing oldies to huddle their frail bodies together for warmth. Who needs cable when you have Withered Oaks TV?

She switches a few of the cameras to thermal mode to better resolve the images of the kids. It's a handy feature that came courtesy of the government. She was supposed to spend the grant dollars upgrading the dining hall, but who the hell will ever notice or care?

While watching the kids, an idea occurs to her. It's likely that nobody knows they're here. This may be the perfect time to take her experiment to the next level. She smiles as giddiness ripples through her body. She walks to the wall behind her desk and presses a hidden switch on its surface. There's a loud hiss of pressure being released, and part of the wall slides open to reveal another room beyond. Eloise steps through the opening into her secret laboratory.

There is a table piled high with assorted electronic parts. There are equipment racks filled with computers and other devices. The room smells of ozone and hums with the noise of cooling fans. Eloise inhales deeply, her anticipation growing. She steps over to a six-foot rack in the corner. This one does not contain equipment. Instead, it houses an oldie. Electronic parts have been grafted onto its papery skin. Its limbs are fitted with biomechanical sheathes to increase strength. Wires and cables protrude from various points on its skull. There's also a Bluetooth device superglued to its temple.

"Time to see what you're really made of."

Eloise removes a feeding tube supplying a gray nutrient base to the thing's stomach. She has more flashes of memory from her childhood, of being forced to care for her grandfather after he got sick. Her mother never bothered to dump him at a nursing home—she was in another country, so what did she care? His soul decayed in rhythm with his body. He stepped up his abuse of Eloise, growing ever more handsy. Eloise shudders, suppresses this latest intrusion into her thoughts.

Eloise is part of a private consortium of researchers attempting to harness and control the magical abilities of oldies. Some scientists theorize that the power of oldies stems from changes that occur in the human brain during aging. So far, Eloise has gained partial control of this oldie's telekinetic abilities, and complete control of its motor functions. Unfortunately, her grafts are only accepted by those with a specific brain type. She uses her creation to sample the brains of incoming residents, hoping to find another compatible subject, but so far has been unsuccessful.

Eloise has made a lot of progress controlling this oldie like a puppet, but what will happen if she commands her creation to kill? How much control does she really have? Now is the perfect time to find out. If her experiment is a success, she can use her creation to seek out and destroy all the world's creepy touchy-feely grandpas.

She moves to one of the computer terminals and types in a few commands. The thing's eyes pop open.

"Make me proud," Eloise says.

Chapter Twelve

Arica and company slink through the hallways, sticking to the shadows. Arica thinks she remembers seeing a records room during her earlier visit, but she's unable to locate it. She doubles back and chooses hallways at random, not willing to admit she has no idea where she's going.

Toby knows Arica is lost, but doesn't want to risk her ire by pointing it out. So, he follows along, occasionally shushing Mary, who has a tendency to hum to herself.

Up ahead, Toby spots movement. He taps Arica's shoulder and gestures in front of them. She reaches out with an arm and pushes them all tight against the wall. She squints, struggling to make out the figures in the poor illumination. From their hunched appearances and slow gaits, they have to be residents. And they appear to be wearing robes. She inches forward to get a better look. They are heading single-file through a doorway that appears to lead to a supply closet. Somehow, they are all fitting inside as though the closet were a clown car.

She spies a figure a head taller than the rest. She would know that shape from anywhere. "Grandpa?"

Toby grabs her wrist and tries to pull her back, but she easily breaks his grip. She steps into the meager light. She's about to call out for Earnest again when a hand covers her mouth and a figure yanks her into the adjoining hallway.

Arica twists and struggles against her captor. She contorts her body in his grip, meets him face-to-face. Wilford braces her against the wall. "Please be quiet. I'm not going to hurt you." Arica grinds her jaw but nods. Wilford slowly removes his hand from her mouth. It smells like old cheese.

Toby weighs the risk/reward ratio of attempting to subdue Wilford, but decides against it.

"What the hell are you kids doing here?" Wilford whispers to them.

"We could ask you the same thing," Arica says.

"I'm here to protect certain business interests. Why are you here?"

"None of your damn—" Arica starts to say.

"She's worried about her grandpa," Toby says. "That's why we're here."

Wilford looks them over, his gaze lingering on Mary for a second. "I think we're all on the same team, here."

"What team is that?" Arica asks.

"The one that wants to stop whatever shit is about to go down tonight."

"What do you mean? What's happening tonight?"

"Did you not see the creepy geriatric monk parade? Those bastards are up to something. Planning a revolt, I'd bet."

"What's a revolt?" Mary asks.

"It's when uppity oldies think they can get the better of us," Wilford says, though there is worry in his voice. "I've overheard things in my time here. The chatter has increased significantly of late. These people truly believe they're destined for some greater purpose. I don't know if they can succeed or not, but I will not have my supply chain disrupted."

Arica narrows her eyes. "Supply chain of what?"

Before Wilford can answer, an odd mechanical sound pierces the darkness. *VAROOOOM CHOONK. VA-ROOOOM CHOONK.*

They all turn to see a figure step out of the shadows. No, not a figure. A monster. Its legs are a nightmarish combination of flesh and pneumatic braces. Skin and metal are fused so well, it's impossible to tell where one ends and the other begins. Tumors and lesions pockmark its face. Blood-red eyes speak of anguish and torture.

Toby steps forward, studying its face. His breathing becomes rapid as he reaches a dreadful, inescapable conclusion. "*Granny?*"

Arica stares at Toby, horrified. "What did you say?"

Toby can't pull his eyes away. He swallows. "Granny, is that you?"

The thing's eyes somehow become even more sad. It opens its mouth and black sludge drips out.

"Holy shit," Arica says. "This is your granny, Bessie?"

Toby doesn't answer. Can't answer.

Wilford steps closer to Bessie. "I've heard this thing roaming the halls, but I've never actually seen it. I always run in the opposite direction." He scratches his head. "What in God's name have they done to you?"

Arica's heart goes out to Toby. No one should have to see a grandparent turned into some kind of biomechanical hell beast. She's about to tell Toby how sorry she is when an invisible force lifts Wilford off the ground, smashes his head into a ceiling tile, and hurls him against the wall. He slides down into a crumpled heap.

"Granny, no!" Toby launches himself at Bessie, his body trembling with fear and anger. Tears stream down his face as he beats his fists against her nightmarish form. She tries to speak, but it comes out as a guttural growl. Toby steps back and wipes his cheeks with the back of his hand. Then he takes off his backpack and unzips it, revealing a plastic bag containing their snacks. With shaky hands, he empties the contents onto the ground before turning back to face what used to be his family. His heart aches as he realizes the mistake they made in bringing Bessie to this cursed place.

"We never should have dumped you here." His words are barely audible above a whisper as he steps behind her and wraps the plastic bag around her face, pulling tightly.

"I'm so sorry," he repeats over and over between sobs.

Arica and Mary watch from a distance. Arica feels she should intervene, but is too stunned to move. Mary can only cry at the tragic scene unfolding before her.

Though Bessie possesses monstrous strength, she makes no attempt to fight back. She tossed Wilford aside like a piece of trash, yet refuses to use her powers on Toby, somehow resisting an unseen influence.

As her oxygen depletes, Bessie's legs give out and she falls to the ground, convulsing and twitching. Toby follows her down, keeping the bag firmly in place, determined to end this nightmare once and for all. A minute later, Bessie goes still. He waits another minute for good measure before finally releasing his grip on the bag.

Arica rushes over and embraces him tightly, her tears mingling with his.

"I... killed my granny," Toby says.

Arica pulls back and looks him in the eye. "Whatever that was, it wasn't your granny."

"What was she trying to say before you put the bag over her head?" Wilford asks as he finally picks himself up, working kinks out of his back. He's going to need a visit to the chiropractor after this.

Toby blinks. "What do you mean?"

"She tried to say something. What was it?"

"I don't know. I'm sure it was some form of *please kill me*."

Wilford shakes his head. "You don't know that. Maybe she was trying to tell you exactly how to disconnect her from whatever was controlling her. Maybe you just murdered your granny for no reason. How will you live with yourself now?"

Arica gasps. "What the fuck is your problem?"

"I'm just telling it like it is."

Arica readies her dick-kicking leg, but then she hears a *woosh* and feels her hair shift as something rushes past her head. She looks up to find a buzzsaw blade embedded in Wilford's gut, the blood soaking through his midsection.

Chapter Thirteen

Wilford glances down at the few metal teeth protruding from his abdomen. The rest of the disc has made a home for itself inside his small intestines. He surprises himself with his lack of emotion. "Huh, would you look at that?"

Arica and Toby spin around to find Eloise standing ten feet away, radiating a murderous fury. She's holding a homemade gun that launches blades fed from a cylindrical compartment above the firing mechanism. Mary cowers against a wall.

Arica points a finger at Eloise. "You're responsible for this abomination? What kind of freak are you?"

Wilford rips the saw blade out of his gut, pulling a not-insignificant portion of his entrails along with it. The blade drops to the floor. He staggers forward, somehow enjoying the blistering pain and sour fecal stench. His intestines trail behind him like a gown of wet, bloody serpents.

"You have no idea what you've done!" Eloise spats. "You've destroyed our only chance at learning to control them. Years of research ruined. Without this technology, the oldies will eventually rise up and kill us all."

"You're insane," Arica cries.

"And you're dead!" Eloise shrieks. She knows that comment sounds dumb, but she's so pissed that she can't think of anything more clever. She points the gun at Arica and pulls the trigger.

Toby shoves Arica to the ground. When she looks up, she sees him standing there, minus one of his arms. The stump spurts an alarming amount of blood. He collapses as Wilford rushes past him.

Wilford grips his intestines, pulls them out a little farther. Eloise fires again, but she is so shocked at the sight of Wilford that the blade goes wide and takes out a plastic ficus. Wilford wraps his intestines around Eloise's neck, intending to strangle her, but they're so slippery that he can't find a decent grip. A length of intestine gets wrapped around Eloise's face. She bites into it, determined to chew her way through. Blood and bile splash against her face.

Arica rushes to Toby's side. "Oh my God, Toby. Why did you do that?"

He smiles weakly. Arica takes his belt off and tries to make a tourniquet, but there's so little meat left below the shoulder that she can't affix it tightly enough. Mary just stares, her eyes quivering.

Wilford and Eloise are tangled up on the floor. He is much larger than her, but is bleeding out quickly. "Go!" he yells at them. "Follow the oldies. Closet leads to the boiler room. Save your friend."

Arica forces Toby to his feet and half drags him down the hallway. For the first time in many years, Arica wants to live. She wants to live so she can save Toby. To make all of this mean something. To feel like she matters. Mary snaps out of her trance and tries to help Arica keep Toby moving.

Wilford passes out and Eloise squirms her way out from underneath him, the smeared blood on the floor acting as a lubricant. She spits out the chewed intestine and wipes fecal slime from her chin. She wipes her hands on her pants and then picks up the gun. She scrambles to her feet, spins on her heels and fires wildly. Despite not aiming, the blade sails down the hall and almost takes off Mary's head. Eloise loads another blade, but the little bastards vanish inside the supply closet before she can get a shot off. She howls with rage and charges after them.

Arica slams the door and locks it. Eloise undoubtedly has a key, but with any luck, she left it in her office. There's another door at the back of the closet that is propped open with a mop bucket. It leads to a set of stairs.

Arica puts her dying friend's remaining arm around her neck. "Come on, Toby. Just a little farther."

He doesn't have the strength to respond.

Arica glances at his sister. "Mary, grab some needles and tape from those bins over there."

Mary does as instructed, then leads the way down the stairs. She goes first, planning to catch her brother if he falls. Luckily, she doesn't have to try, because Arica makes it to the bottom of the stairs without losing control of him.

They're in a drab, concrete room with large machinery. A row of hot-water pipes runs down the back wall. Arica drags Toby to the nearest pipe. "I'm so sorry. This is going to hurt."

With her arms around his waist, she heaves him onto the scalding pipe. His stump sizzles and pops as the heat from the boiler cooks his flesh. Toby lets out a primal scream. Arica pulls him off, but some of the flesh sticks to the pipe and his stump continues to ooze blood. The pipe isn't hot enough to instantly cauterize the wound, so she throws him back onto the pipe and his screams start anew. Soon they fade to a whimper and he passes out.

The smell of charred meat floods Arica's nostrils. She pulls him off the pipe again and is relieved to find the bleeding has almost entirely stopped. But Toby's face is ashen, and Arica knows he won't survive long without a transfusion.

"Mary, get over here. You want to save your brother, right?"

Eloise did not in fact forget her keys, but she has so damn many of them on her ring that she can't find which one is for the supply closet. The metal jingles as she sifts through the keys furiously. Her hands cannot find what her brain knows is there. She had the opportunity to upgrade to electronic locks years ago, but of course, she funneled the money elsewhere. And her obsessive need for control means she keeps keys for all doors on her at all times.

She has to go through the ring a second time before she finally finds the one that works. "Stupid piece of shit key!"

She flings the door open and rushes into the closet, still wearing Wilford's intestines. Lots of blood on the floor. *Good.* She steps around it and then heads down the stairs at the back of the closet, carefully navigating the blood-slick steps. When she reaches the bottom, her face scrunches as she takes in the scene.

Toby is lying on his back. A rubber tube is taped to the boy's wrist. The other end is attached to the bloody girl's neck. Also, the room smells like barbecue.

"Oh, child," Eloise says. "There isn't nearly enough blood in your tiny little body to save him."

Arica steps out from her hiding spot in the shadows. Holding a giant wrench in her hands, she swings it at Eloise, aiming for her head. But Arica doesn't have enough strength to lift the wrench high enough, so it connects instead with Eloise's neck with a sickening crunch. Eloise's makeshift gun clatters to the floor and her on top of it.

Eyes flashing with anger, Arica drops the wrench, leans over and reaches underneath Eloise. Her hand wraps around the handle of the buzzsaw gun. "Mary can replace her own blood." Arica's lips curl in a sardonic smile. "But bitch, you can't." She pulls the trigger and a blade slices into Eloise's chest cavity, shredding a lung. Blood spreads like a pool of motor oil on the dark cement. Already paralyzed from the neck down, Eloise can do nothing but choke on her own blood.

Chapter Fourteen

After entering the boiler room, Cornelius had led the oldies through a hidden door leading to a cave. "It's here, just as Mr. Fuzzles promised," he said. After following the cave deep into the earth, they finally emerge into a cavern the size of a high school gym.

If Earnest has been in a weirder place in his lifetime, he can't think of it now. Columns of meaty, translucent tendons run from floor to ceiling. They twitch and quiver in sync with each other. Attached to the tendons at various heights are elastic membranes stretched tight like trampolines. And on a ledge above a sump pool is something resembling a giant face growing out of the rock. The skin is gray and cracked with slashes of neon yellow. Two orbs like polished coal serve as its eyes. They roll slowly in their sockets, observing the newcomers. Cornelius lights torches around the cavern. When he finishes, he takes his place next to Earnest. They are flanked by Snapdragon, Milton, Pierre, and Daddy Suckface. Dozens of others in pastel robes stand patiently alongside them.

Cornelius lifts his hands in the air. "Oh, mighty Mr. Fuzzles. We have answered your call. Please deliver us from those who would so callously forsake us. Lend us your guidance and allow us to be your holy vessels, your instruments of destruction. Together we shall unleash the Curse of Ages."

Cornelius' voice reaches a crescendo. "Praise be to Mr. Fuzzles! All hail Mr. Fuzzles!"

"Hail, Mr. Fuzzles," echoes the crowd.

Mr. Fuzzles does not respond. Cornelius thinks he may not be laying it on thick enough.

"Oh, magnificent one, we cry out to you from the depths of our tortured souls. No one but you can save us from this unholy place. We have done penance, and we place our fate in your hands. You have called us here for a reason." His voice vibrates throughout the cavern, resonating with pent-up emotion. "What would you have us do?"

As he waits for a response, his heart pounds in his chest. The silence deepens, and he struggles to control his breathing. "You are a savior to old people." He shakes uncontrollably, claws at his robe. "We are not worthy of you." He spreads his arms wide as though willing himself to be filled with divine energy. "Please tell me. Your servant begs this soul-crushing agony to end." Tears stream down his face, dripping onto dirt and rock. "Goddamn it, answer me! Speak! How can I serve you?"

Reflections of flame dance in those black eyes. DID YOU BRING THE MARSHMALLOWS?

They don't hear the voice so much as it suddenly appears in their heads. Earnest realizes Cornelius is right about Mr. Fuzzles being telepathic. *Neat.*

Cornelius sighs with relief. "Yes, Great Master." He snaps his fingers and Pierre produces a bag of marshmallows from under his robe. Cornelius takes it, then walks around the sump pool to a slope that leads up to the ledge. He walks slowly but deliberately, savoring every moment of this holiest of times. Cornelius knew of his lord's sweet tooth. He had attempted to honor it in the past by taking a few of the residents, stuffing them with sugary treats, and sacrificing them in the name of Mr. Fuzzles. But now, they can feed the Great Master directly.

He reaches the top and steps up to the face of Mr. Fuzzles. It's twice as tall as Cornelius. The rocky flesh splits open and a glorious maw extends forward. It is filled with a bright, syrupy red liquid, like the kind used for snow cones. Cornelius tears open the package of marshmallows and dumps them into the maw. As they dissolve into the liquid, Cornelius feels waves of rapture emanating from Mr. Fuzzles. Cornelius lets Mr. Fuzzles have this moment and returns to stand with his comrades.

"Is he going to be okay?" Mary cries.

Arica nods as she removes the blood tube from Toby. "Don't worry, your brother's going to be just fine." She has no clue if Mary is even a match for Toby's blood type, or if Mary's blood curse would be an issue. But Arica had to try something. Some of his color has returned, but his breathing is raspy and shallow. She reaches into the backpack and pulls out the tube of gum salve she got from the clambake. She lathers it on Toby's crispy stump.

Arica pulls out her phone and hands it to Mary. "I don't have a signal here. I need you to take this and go outside and call 911. Can you do that for me, Mary?"

Mary glances at her brother.

"He'll be okay," Arica says. "But you need to make that call right now."

"What about you?"

"I'm going after my grandpa and the others. I have to know what they're up to."

"But there's nobody here."

Arica gestures toward a spot on the far wall. "There has to be a hidden door over there. That's where all the dusty footprints end. Now, you have to hurry! Toby is counting on you."

Arica expects a protest, but Mary nods her head. *Good girl.*

Mary stands and hands over her Super Soaker. "Take this, just in case."

Arica smiles. "Okay."

Mary turns and runs for the stairs. Arica straps the Super Soaker behind her back and picks up Eloise's buzzsaw gun. She heads to the back of the room where, sure enough, a door hides.

"Arica?"

She turns. Toby has opened his eyes. She runs over. "Hey, how are you feeling?"

"Terrible. I think I'm dying."

"You're not dying. I won't let you."

"Take care of Mary, for me."

Arica holds his hand. "Look, if we make it out of here, we'll go out someplace nice. Alright? Just the two of us."

"You mean like a date?"

"Yes, a date," she lies. "But you have to survive first."

"Okay. I can do that," he says, then closes his eyes again.

The residents wait patiently for Mr. Fuzzles to finish his marshmallows. When he looks like he's finally done, Cornelius says, "Now, my lord, please bless us with the secret behind the Curse of Ages."

WHICH OF YOU VOLUNTEERS?

Earnest shoots his hand in the air. "I do!" He doesn't know what he's volunteering for, but he's going to make his life mean something one way or another. Cornelius gives him side-eye.

COME TO ME.

Earnest hesitates, then walks around the sump pool and up the slope until he is face to face with Mr. Fuzzles. One of Great Master's black eyes transforms into an inky liquid, held in place by some invisible force. Earnest feels compelled to place his arm inside. He gingerly pushes his hand past the pitch-black surface. The black liquid moves around his hand, caressing it like a newborn cub. The liquid feels warm and gooey, like being embraced by a womb.

THE LINK IS MADE.

Earnest's head explodes with images from Mr. Fuzzles. He can't make sense of it all, but he knows that Mr. Fuzzles was abandoned by his kind eons ago. They left this planet and refused to take him along. Earnest feels the hurt and the anger and the fear and the terror. An infinite pit of despair. Earnest's soul weeps for Mr. Fuzzles. Now Earnest understands why Mr. Fuzzles wants to join forces with them. They share a common goal of punishing people who abandon others.

FROM THIS CONDUIT, I SHALL LINK WITH YOU ALL.

A ribbon of black lightning erupts from Earnest's chest and sears the air. It strikes the nearest cavern tendril and splinters into dozens of bolts, each arcing to another tendril and then to the robed figures. The cavern is alive with chaos and energy. Earnest's blood sings with joy. He has never felt such power. Together, there is nothing that can stop them. The world stands before them like a banquet, ready to be eaten. Earnest laughs with uncontrollable bliss.

NOW YOU SHALL LEARN THE SECRET.

Cornelius can barely contain his excitement. The power he feels is as thrilling as it is intoxicating. The oldies cheer as the black lightning crackles all around. Cornelius beckons them to quiet down, then addresses Mr. Fuzzles. "Yes, Great Master. What is it? What is the Curse of Ages? What vengeance shall be wrought on the young?"

THE CURSE IS . . .

This is it, Cornelius thinks. The moment he's been waiting on for so long.

MAGIC THAT WILL DRAIN THEIR BANK ACCOUNTS.

Cornelius looks down, squints, then looks back at Mr. Fuzzles. "I'm sorry. What was that? Their bank accounts?"

YES, THEIR BANK ACCOUNTS.

"What does that mean, their bank accounts?"

WE WILL DRAIN THEM.

"And. . . then what?"

THEY WILL BE BESIEGED WITH OVERDRAFT FEES.

Snapdragon throws off his hood. "What the fuck are you saying, man? Their fucking bank accounts? That's what all this is about?"

WE WILL CONTROL ALL WEALTH. ARE YOU NOT PLEASED?

"No, I am not pleased!" Snapdragon cries. "You promised us revenge. Where's the blood? Where's the carnage?"

Cornelius steps forward. "Great Master, what my friend means is that bankrupting the young isn't what we had in mind."

"Where the hell am I?" Milton asks.

HUMANS CARE ONLY FOR MONEY.

"Well. . ." Cornelius peers up at Earnest through the curtain of black lightning.

Earnest tries to figure out if he should explain to Mr. Fuzzles how ruining the economy could backfire, but he's too busy trying to sort out which thoughts belong to him and which belong to the creature whose eyeball his arm is currently submerged in. And Earnest is pretty sure he's jizzed himself three times since he touched Mr. Fuzzles, which is exactly three more times than he has in the past five years.

Chapter Fifteen

When Arica enters the cavern, she is greeted by a chaotic combination of the grotesque and the absurd. Bolts of black electricity rebound between columns of sinewy flesh. They spring off and arc between hunched-over oldies looking like so many Easter eggs.

She also sees what looks like her grandfather up on a ledge being devoured by a sentient rock demon. Earnest has a stupid smile plastered on his face. She figures the demon must be controlling him somehow. She aims the buzzsaw gun right at the creature and fires. The blade travels the length of the cavern, slices through the creature's hideous cheek, and disappears within. The pain and confusion weaken its grip on Earnest, whose thoughts clear. He notices his granddaughter standing near the entrance to the cavern. "Arica?"

I AM BETRAYED.

The cavern rumbles, tossing oldies to the ground. The walls of the cavern ripple and undulate. Gray powder falls from the ceiling like snow. Two-meter-long creatures burst from the surrounding walls. Hard like charcoal, the arachnid-like beasts free themselves from their rocky entombment and attack the oldies.

A creature boils out of the wall a few feet from Arica. Segmented like a spider with the legs of a centipede, the creature has greenish-purple hexagons that fade to yellow at the edges. Orange antennas quiver next to its candy-red fangs, black pincer claws glistening below them.

Arica points the gun at the . . . spiderpede? She steadies her aim and fires. The blade pierces its abdomen and black liquid erupts from the wound. Unfazed, the creature charges forward. Unable to reload in time, Arica desperately shoves the barrel downward into the creature's face. She stops the beast's momentum, but its fangs grab onto the barrel with unbelievable strength. Arica tries to reload, but the fangs rip the weapon from her hands. She takes off running into the middle of the oldies. Safety in numbers, after all.

As Earnest watches the scene unfold, he realizes the horrible truth. Mr. Fuzzles is using Earnest's own demon-summoning powers against them. "Why are you doing this?" he asks Mr. Fuzzles.

But Mr. Fuzzles is done talking. All Earnest senses from him now is rage. He can also feel something behind the rage. Surging heat like a brilliant star. The source of the being's power. Earnest needs to find it. He's a foolish old man who has made a terrible mistake, and now his granddaughter may die because of him.

He pushes his arm deeper inside Mr. Fuzzles. It feels like gelatin filled with chunks of warm mud. He pushes harder, running his fingers through strands of the monster's brain tissue. The hot, sticky meat pulses between his fingers. He finds something hard and unmoving buried deep in the brain. He pushes against it, but nothing happens. He strains harder, then it suddenly cracks like an egg. His arm sinks even deeper into Mr. Fuzzles' brain, and he wraps his hand around a small object with a smooth, glassy texture. Warmth oozes into his palm and up his forearm. He pulls, but the object is stuck fast. He shoves his other arm inside the eye and works feverishly to free the object.

The residents of Withered Oaks did not come unprepared. As soon as the horrific creatures showed themselves, various weapons appeared from under robes, including baseball bats, crowbars, tasers, and cans of mace. They didn't know what to expect upon meeting Mr. Fuzzles, but they were hoping it would involve taking to the streets and rioting.

Daddy Suckface swallows a spiderpede whole and laughs as it chews its way out of him. Pierre launches leg curses at the spiderpedes, pulverizing their limbs and causing them to trip over themselves. With each curse, a new wart erupts on the surface of his skin.

One of the oldies is impaled on the fangs of a spiderpede. He drops his bat, which rolls to Arica's feet. She snatches it up and bashes the creature over the head. It releases the oldie and grabs the bat, splintering it to pieces. The beast lunges for Arica but she dodges to the side, passing through one of the black lightning bolts. It arcs and spits all around her, but she seems unaffected by it.

Snapdragon appears next to her, wielding a can of mace and a taser. He uses them simultaneously on the spiderpede. The beast goes rigid, flips onto its back and twitches uncontrollably. Pierre grabs a torch and sets the thing on fire.

"Thanks for the backup," Arica says.

Snapdragon winks at her and then looks for other targets. Several of the oldies are overcome and devoured by spiderpedes. Snapdragon uses the flames of the burning spiderpede to augment his own abilities. Fireballs shoot forth from his hands. He blankets the frontline of the hideous beasts with fiery death.

Arica needs to get to her grandfather. She waits for an opening, then charges around the sump pool and runs up the sloping path. Two spiderpedes drop from the ceiling, trapping her in between. She considers diving into the sump pool, but it's so shallow she's liable to crack her skull.

The spiderpedes scuttle toward her with fangs clicking. In a desperate move, Arica pulls the Super Soaker from behind her back. It's a useless, plastic thing, but she brought it because she knew it would make Mary happy. She aims it at one of the spiderpedes and pulls the trigger, hoping to distract it long enough that she can get past. A stream of Mary's cursed blood shoots forth and sprays the thing in the mouth. Then, the most curious thing happens. The spiderpede pops like a balloon. Chunks of rocky flesh with spiny hairs rain down upon her. Without pausing, Arica whips around and sprays the other spiderpede. Same result—an explosion of blood, hair, and spindly legs.

She runs the rest of the way up the ledge. "Grandpa, are you okay?" It takes everything she has to be heard over the cacophony.

"Oh, I'm fine. Why do you ask?"

"You're elbow-deep in that thing's eyes."

"Don't worry about me. I know what I'm doing. Go help the others."

Arica decides to trust that Earnest knows what he's doing, despite appearances to the contrary. She turns and races back down the path, spraying every spiderpede she can find. They all explode on contact. The oldies cheer as the tide of battle turns. There are only a few spiderpedes left by the time Arica runs dry. She drops the Super Soaker and picks up a crowbar to help finish off the others, but suddenly, the remaining spiderpedes go limp and the lightning ceases.

Piss-yellow light bathes the cavern. It shimmers off the walls like the reflection of a pool that too many kids swam in. Arica looks up to find her grandpa standing on the ledge, holding an iridescent crystal in his hands.

"Mr. Fuzzles is dead," he announces.

Cornelius limps forward, his leg bloodied. His eyes are bulging out of his body, the increased vision having made it easier to fight the spiderpedes. "I don't understand. What went wrong?"

"What went wrong," Arica says, "is that you and your little cult buddies dragged the wrong man into your schemes. My grandpa is way too smart for that. I agree that society needs to change, but this is not the way."

Earnest's expression sours. The momentary remorse he felt evaporates. "Mr. Fuzzles might not have had the best plan, but his heart was in the right place."

"His heart?" Arica says. "That *thing*—whatever it was—had no heart. It's foolish and misguided to think otherwise."

"Misguided?" Earnest says. He addresses the entire group: "I'll tell you what's misguided. Believing senior citizens have nothing to offer. That our decades of experience are of no value to younger generations. That we should be squashed like bugs under Chuck Taylors and fat Nikes." He points at Arica, finger dripping with vitreous humor. "You say we're misguided. I say we're backed into a corner and are tired of putting up with your condescending bullshit, and now it's time to pay the price."

Earnest shoves the crystal in his mouth and gulps it down.

Before Arica can react, the black lightning starts up again, even stronger than before.

"Mr. Fuzzles lacked imagination," Earnest says, his voice booming through the cavern. "He may have failed us, but I assure you, I will not."

Arica asks, "Grandpa, what the hell do you think you're doing?" but he can't hear her.

Earnest forms an idea, and he pours the collective magics of the Withered Oaks residents into it. He feels it swell and swell until he can contain it no longer, then he lets the power explode outward in a wave of pure, focused energy. Arica screams as the world goes dark.

Chapter Sixteen

Julie sits at her dining room table, admiring her spread. Espresso crepes with dark chocolate sauce, eggs benedict, glazed Irish bacon, lemon blueberry scones, and yogurt parfait. She takes several photos and posts them on her social media accounts. *Airing the old man stench out of my house! #finallyfree #ditchedthedad #hopeheeatsshit.*
 She sets her phone down and grabs a piece of bacon. She takes a bite and shivers with delight as her mouth explodes with flavor, the grease coating her tongue. Never has breakfast tasted sweeter. She thinks about waking up Arica, but Julie wants to revel in this moment a little longer. She kicked Mark—the guy she met at the clambake—out before sunrise so she could have this morning to herself. What a special time this is—her first breakfast without her dad intruding on her space. She imagines Earnest waking up at Withered Oaks to reconstituted eggs and moldy toast.
 "More than he deserves," she mutters.
 A knock at the door interrupts her reverie. Did someone order a package? She takes a sip of coffee, walks to the door and opens it. Her jaw goes slack when she sees Earnest standing there. He's wearing a hideous bathrobe covered in blood and viscera. His mouth opens with a devious smile, eyes glowing like hot coals. The skin on his face and exposed arms crackles with black sparks. Julie sitcom-slaps herself.
 "I assure you, I'm quite real," Earnest says.

"How did you... Why are you here?"

"Mind if I come in?"

Earnest steps past her into the dining room.

"It's strange," he says. "Yesterday, all I wanted was to come home to this house. Now, the thought of living with you is revolting. I'm afraid you're going to have to leave. Arica can stay, if she wants."

"Excuse me? You can't kick me out of my own house. And what the hell is wrong with your eyes?"

Earnest turns to face her. "Are you forgetting? The house is still in my name."

Julie shakes her head. "This is absurd. The deed is just a formality. No oldie ever challenges ownership."

"I'll give you a week to pack up your shit. But don't worry, you'll find another place to live. I suspect several facilities are about to experience a vacancy crisis." Earnest shoves a slice of bacon from Julie's plate into his mouth and chews.

"How dare you speak to me like this! Arica and I will not stand for it. You hear me? Arica will talk some sense into you." She turns her head toward the hallway. "Arica!"

"She's not here," Earnest says, washing the bacon down with a gulp of Julie's coffee.

"What do you mean, she's not here? Of course she's here. Arica!"

"She's recuperating at the hospital. Exhaustion, they say. She'll be fine. Did the doctors not explain any of this?"

Julie had turned her phone off, as she didn't want to be disturbed. "I don't know, I've been busy."

"I'm going to take a shower and then go visit her."

"No, you're not, mister. You're going to march yourself straight back to—" Julie grunts and grabs her stomach. Her muscles knot and clench violently, bones popping. It feels like she's being torn apart from the inside.

"There's something else I should mention," Earnest says. "National Dump Off Your Old People Day is no more. I'm seeing to that. From its ashes comes NYPGWTFDD—National Young People Get What They Fucking Deserve Day."

Julie doubles over, gasping for breath. She vomits bacon and coffee. The skin on the back of her neck down past her calves becomes rigid and calcified and rips through her clothes.

"I'm sparing the children because they're innocent in all this. They just believe what they're told. But people like you should know better."

Julie holds her trembling hands in front of her. The skin turns gray and slimy. Her fingers fuse together. "Please, stop," she tries to say, but gurgles up salt water instead. Her body collapses in on itself, forming a chunk of yellowish-orange clam meat surrounded by shell. Embedded in the meat are two human eyeballs.

Earnest crouches in front of the Julie clam. "I need you to hear what I'm saying, Daughter."

Her goopy eyes fixate on him, pupils dilating.

"You've had your fun, but now it's over. Every year on this day, you will transform into a clam to remind you of your sins. You become that which you used to celebrate your cruelty."

Cornelius and Snapdragon enter from outside. They help Earnest pick up the Julie clam and carry her out the door. They shove her in the back of what was once Wilford's van. Next to her is Julie's boyfriend Mark, who has also been transformed into a clam.

Pierre drives the lot of them to the local garbage heap. They dump the clams in a pile of food scraps, cracked rubber hoses, soiled bags, and broken glass.

"How long are they going to be like that?" Cornelius asks.

"Three or four hours," Earnest says.

"Wicked, dude. I want to be here when they change back just to see the looks on their faces."

Earnest shakes his head. "We still have work to do."

"Like what?" asks Cornelius.

"I'm going to get myself elected president. Then I can formally put an end to places like Withered Oaks."

Snapdragon looks at Earnest askance. "How are you going to get people to vote for you?"

"Easy," Earnest says. "They'll elect me out of fear of further retribution. I now have the powers of Mr. Fuzzles at my disposal."

As they watch, the Mark clam shoots a fountain of jizz toward the Julie clam. She opens her bivalve and siphons down the sperm to her awaiting eggs.

"Fuckin' gross," Snapdragon says.

Chapter Seventeen

Several years later...

Arica glides into the Roosevelt Room, Toby following closely. He carries a tablet with his prosthetic arm, using his remaining hand to type. Arica scoots a chair back and sinks into the soft, chestnut leather. The chair is impeccably spotless and smells of lemon cleaning solution. Toby takes a seat beside her.

"Are you sure you want me here?" he asks. "I'm only an assistant."

"It'll sound better coming from you."

"Your grandfather hates me."

"He doesn't hate you. He just thinks—"

Snapdragon strolls into the room, talking loudly on his phone.

"You goddamn well better get it done!" he spits into the phone. "Otherwise, *you* can explain to the president why you're missing the deadline. If you're lucky, he'll just turn you into a goldfish and flush you down the toilet the next time he takes a shit!"

He ends the call and sits down opposite Arica and Toby at the conference table.

"Sorry about that," Snapdragon says. "We're kicking out a bunch of tech bros from some fancy condos and converting them into senior living. Who knew being Secretary of Elder Housing would involve busting so many balls?"

Arica sits back, the leather creaking. "Young people need places to live, too."

The cords in his neck stiffen. "Well, duh. We're resettling them at places like Withered Oaks, where we can keep an eye on them." He crosses his arms, his black t-shirt showing off his tats, now full sleeves, orange-red flames licking his biceps.

"But they need to be close to urban centers where the jobs are."

"Most of these assholes work remotely."

Cornelius enters the room, chomping on a cream cheese bagel. Part of his eye goop drips onto the bagel, adding to the flavor. "This better be important," he says through a mouthful. "I've got some textbooks to approve." He takes a seat to the right of Snapdragon.

"Yeah, what the hell are we even doing here?" Snapdragon asks.

"I'll explain when my grandfather gets here," Arica says.

They spend a couple minutes in silence, staring at each other.

"How's your sister, Toby?" Cornelius asks.

Toby looks up, startled. "Mary's fine. She got another job supplying blood for a horror movie. *S&M Spiders From Hell*, or some such."

"Now, see, I would totally watch that," Snapdragon says. "Creatures, death, sex. It's a family night."

Earnest saunters into the room and takes his place at the head of the table. "Sorry I'm late."

"We were—" Arica says.

"I'm just kidding. I'm not sorry at all. I'm the goddamn president." He bobs his head back and forth like a rooster.

Arica sighs. As Earnest's power has increased, so have his microaggressions. He's become increasingly overbearing and hostile over the years. He made Pierre the Secretary of State in order to negotiate more favorable trade deals. If the head of another state pushes back, Pierre threatens to break their legs. And with all the cursing he's been doing, Pierre's skin is completely knotted over with pus-oozing warts, making him an intimidating figure.

"You want to tell us why we're here, Arica?" Earnest asks while examining his fingernails. "Or do you want to continue wasting my time?"

Arica digs her fingers into the armrests. She can tell Toby's too terrified to speak, so she takes the tablet from him and examines her notes.

"We're here because I want to talk about all the complaints we've been fielding."

Earnest huffs, looks to Snapdragon and Cornelius. "Here we go again, boys."

Arica continues, "Ever since your declaration that older citizens can't be charged for using their powers in a criminal manner, they've become increasingly bold. Just yesterday, an old couple in Cleveland turned a shopkeeper into a slug over a dispute involving the price of tomatoes."

"I like their style," Earnest says.

"Then they poured salt on him."

Earnest chuckles.

Arica slams the table with her fist. "This is important, Grandpa! They're learning this behavior from you. They watch you transform people you disagree with into nonhuman creatures, and they feel they can do the same."

Earnest leans toward her dangerously, blood pressure rising. "Watch your tone with me, Arica. And you'll address me as Mr. President."

Arica stares back, defiantly. She's never gotten used to the black sparks that crawl over his cracked, pockmarked skin like an army of bullet ants.

She says, "I asked Snapdragon and Cornelius to come because I think the Department of Elder Housing and the Department of Re-education can help us here. We need to teach people they're safe in their own homes, and that young people are not a threat to them."

"Whoa, don't drag us into this," Snapdragon says, holding up his hands. Cornelius nods. They would rather be anywhere than in this room at the moment. Toby squirms, tries to keep from passing out.

Earnest tries to control his breathing. He doesn't want to make an example out of Arica, but he will if he has to. He's hyper-aware of anyone who tries to take advantage of him. When he speaks, he does so in a measured tone: "You are sticking your nose where it does not belong, Arica. When you came to me wanting to start a national suicide prevention initiative, I gave you this job so you could do just that. Not so you could challenge my decisions, especially not in front of others."

Arica swallows hard. "There's something else. People are calling for the end of NYPGWTFDD. They say they've learned their lesson and are tired of being turned into clams every year."

Earnest snorts. "NYPGWTFDD is not only the best holiday, it's a great acronym. Really rolls off the tongue."

"It's disruptive to the economy. And when they're clams, they all have sex with each other. I have eight new siblings from three different fathers, and those numbers will continue to increase."

Everyone bursts out laughing except for Arica and Toby.

"It's causing overpopulation," Arica presses.

Earnest stops laughing, sniffs and wipes the tears from his eyes. "I've got that all figured out. Remember those shadow labs we shut down that were experimenting with old people, turning them into cyborgs and whatnot?"

Arica nods warily. Toby lowers his head in remembrance of his granny.

"Well, they're just sitting there unused," Earnest says. "I say we open them back up, stuff them with young people, and do experiments on them. We can test new dementia drugs. Rip all their teeth out and evaluate the latest in denture technology. See which artificial hearts actually work."

"Oh! We could harvest their organs and shit," Snapdragon says. He and Cornelius high-five each other. Arica clutches her tablet to her chest, horrified.

"And you," Earnest says, pointing at Arica, "As the head of Health and Human Services, you're going to be in charge of making sure these experiments run smoothly. I want you to call your staff and make the arrangements to get this program underway."

"I will *not!*" Arica cries, jumping out of her seat. "This is beyond wrong. I will not be a party to it."

Toby doubles over, hyperventilating. No one pays him any mind. Earnest says, "Oh, but you will be a party to it. Because if you don't, I'll use my powers to make their lives even worse than they are now. You think NYPGWTFDD is bad? What if I make it last for a month instead of a day? What if I curse everyone with flesh-eating bacteria, starting with Toby?"

Earnest cocks his head toward Toby, who screams and falls backward in his chair, tumbling to the ground. Arica drops her tablet, goes to her knees and flips Toby onto his back. He writhes in agony as pustules erupt over his face, reddish-black like rotting apples. "Stop this!" Arica cries, trying to hold Toby down to prevent him from hurting himself.

"Of course," Earnest says. He waves his hand, and the pustules cease their growth. "Call your staff, or I'll come back and finish the job." He stands and turns toward the door, motioning for Snapdragon and Cornelius to follow. They get up slowly and follow Earnest out, refusing eye contact with Arica.

Arica holds Toby's hand as he winces in pain. "I'm so sorry, Toby. I never thought he would go this far. I should have left him to die in that cavern."

"Not your fault," Toby says. "Don't call your staff. We can go away somewhere where he can't find us. You can't give in to him. You—" His voice trails off in a coughing spurt.

Arica's face slackens. "I'll get you some help," she says absently. She stands, ambles out of the room in a daze. In the hallway, she hears muffled laughter from the Oval Office. Probably at her and Toby's expense. She grabs the nearest intern and tells him to go get the onsite doctor. She thinks about her staff, whether she can bring herself to do what her grandfather wants. Then she thinks of Toby lying on the floor of the Roosevelt Room, and of her siblings, some of whom she has yet to meet. She takes out her phone and calls her staff, hating herself through the entire discussion.

Afterward, she slumps onto a bench, dejected. Earnest emerges from the Oval Office, along with Cornelius and Snapdragon. Earnest stops in front of Arica while Cornelius and Snapdragon keep walking, heads down. They almost run into Toby as he's being wheeled out of the Roosevelt Room on a gurney.

"I never properly thanked you," Earnest says to Arica.

She lifts her head. Earnest's hair has regained its black sheen, and his skin now appears frozen in time. Arica wonders if Earnest will live forever with that cursed crystal inside of him. Mr. Fuzzles was thousands of years old.

"Thank me for what?"

"For helping me dispatch Mr. Fuzzles. Couldn't have done it without you." He gives her a playful jab to the shoulder. He actually thinks he would have killed Mr. Fuzzles and taken his power regardless if Arica hadn't crashed the party. But he knows the importance of propping up your slaves from time to time.

"You're my grandpa. I would do anything for you."

Earnest smiles as they both pretend the sentiment is true. Arica's phone pings. "I need to take this," she says without looking at the screen.

"I'll let you get to it. You're doing a great job, Arica. I'm so proud to have you as a granddaughter." He turns and strolls off.

Arica gives the barest sneer, then checks her phone. There's a text from Mary. She sent a link to an article along with the message, "*Have u seen this??*" Arica taps on the link. It's an Associated Press story about a sinkhole that opened up on a preschool playground and swallowed an entire class. An oldie who lives across the street claimed responsibility. Said he was tired of all the noise. But even though the teacher was killed, the children all survived without a scratch. The only thing the kids have in common is that they were all conceived on NYPGWTFDD by clam sex.

Arica feels a surge of something she hasn't felt in a long time—hope. She decides her next vacation will be a trip back home. It's time she gets to know her new siblings.

About the Author

John Chambers is the author of *Cold War*, *Scourge Ship*, and *Humiliation Nation*, all of which are classic works of literature and definitely not cries for help.
You can find John's stuff at linktr.ee/jcbizarro. He also has a blog he rarely updates at chambersofdelight.com.

Other Titles from Planet Bizarro

Peculiar Monstrosities – *A Bizarre Horror Anthology*
Extremely Bizarre – *A Bizarro Extreme Horror Anthology*
The Best of Bizarro Fiction: Volume 1 – *A Bizarro Anthology*
The Best of Bizarro Fiction: Volume 2 - *A Bizarro Anthology*
Sons of Sorrow *by Matthew A. Clarke*
Porn Land *by Kevin Shamel*
Russells in Time *by Kevin Shamel*
Weird Fauna of the Multiverse *A trio of novellas by Leo X. Robertson*
A Quaint New England Town *by Gregory L. Norris*
Selleck's 'Stache is Missing! *by Charles Chadwick*
Songs About My Father's Crotch *by Dustin Reade*
The Secret Sex Lives of Ghosts *by Dustin Reade*
Valley of the Frankensteins *by Dustin Reade*
Better Call Rob *by Dustin Reade*
Dad Jokes *by Justin Hunter*
The Falling Crystal Palace *by Carl Fuerst*

Dead Monkey Rum *by Robert Guffey*
Ebola Saves the Planet! and Other Wholesome Tales *by Matthew A. Clarke*
Troll *by Matthew A. Clarke*
Backdoor Carnivore *by G.G.Gilt*
Jesus of Scumburg *by Leo X. Robertson*
Cthulhu Fishing off the Iraq Nebula *by Chris Meekings*
My Weird Nightmare Baby *by Riley Odell*
Scanlon's Overpass *by William Higgs III*
Warped Brood *by Kevin Stadt*
Interviews with the Temporally Displaced *by Shawn Wayne Langhans*
Strawberry Jelly Donut Creem Betweens: A Full Review *by Mike James Davis*
All I Want is to Take Shrooms and Listen to the Color of Nazi Screams *by John Baltisberger*
Shithole USA *by Mark Zirbel*
Cyberpunk Zombie Jihad: The Expanded Edition *by Mark Zirbel*
Fate is Fuzzy *by Elias Van Zimmer*
Cold War *by John Chambers*
Cursing Home *by John Chambers*
Stone Ovaries and Bowling Balls Trapped in Beautiful Prodigy World *by Douglas J. Ogurek*
Snailbutter *by Ben Fitts*
My Birth and Other Regrets *by Ben Fitts*

Milton Keynes UK
Ingram Content Group UK Ltd.
UKHW041136081124
450823UK00008B/40